TOTALLY ENGAGED

SIX 32 CENTRAL #4

MINA V. ESGUERRA

BRIGHT GIRL BOOKS

Cover designed by Tania Arpa

Photo shoot directed by Chi Yu Rodriguez (RomanceClass Covers)

CONTENT NOTE

This story is set in 2019, and the year is mentioned in the text. There is a complicated mother/daughter relationship portrayed on the page.

This book is heat level 3 and follows #romanceclass guidelines requiring HEA/HFN for romance.

#romanceclass community heat levels:

0 - No sex on or off the page

1 - Off-page sex mentioned in story

2 - At least one "Closed door" sex scene

3 - At least one "Open door" sex scene

4 - "Open door" sex scenes, erotic romance elements, with HEA

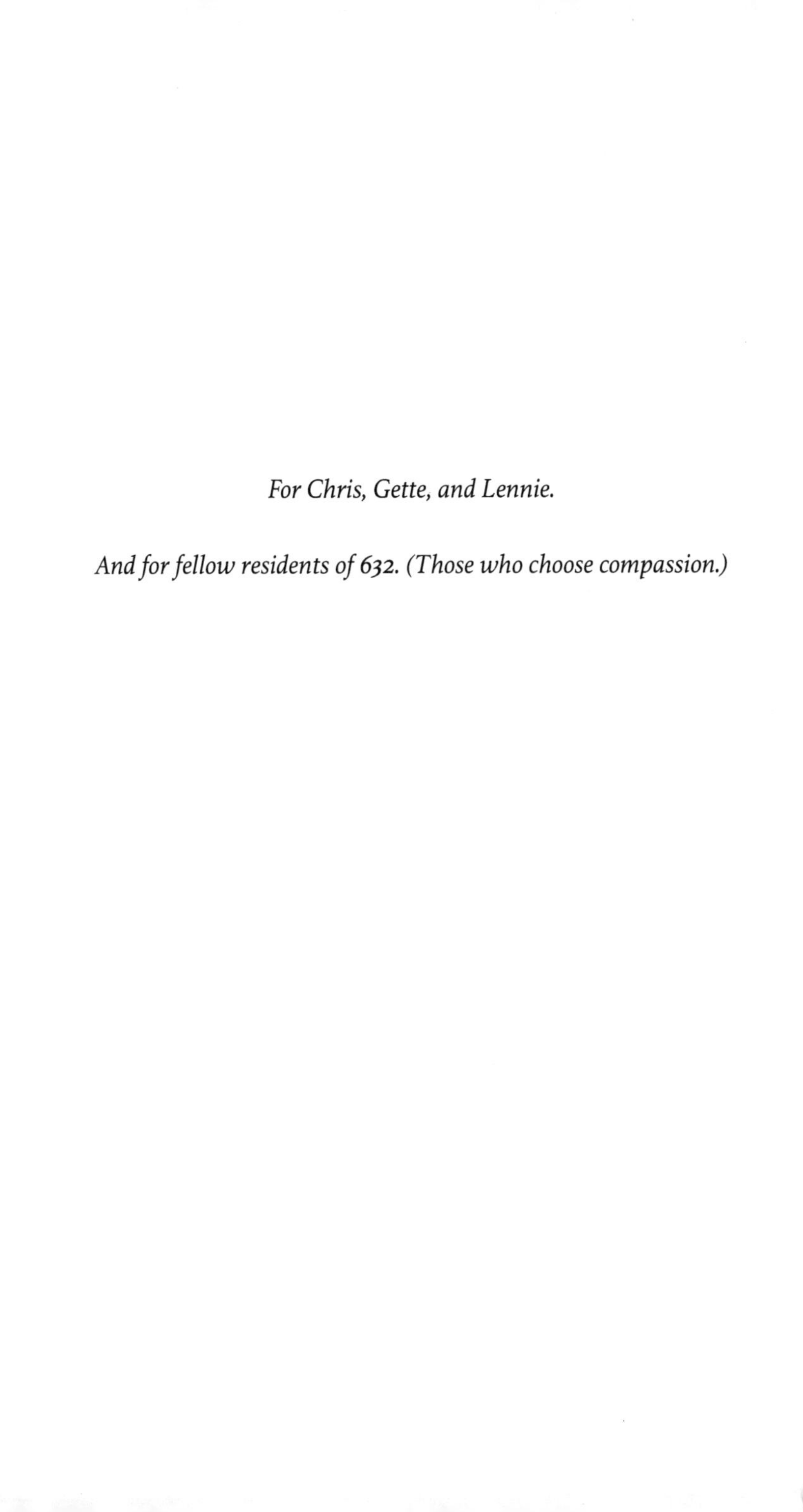

For Chris, Gette, and Lennie.

And for fellow residents of 632. (Those who choose compassion.)

1

W*ell, that can't be him.*

Oh no. It is.

Oh no, Tana's brother is gorgeous.

What an absolute betrayal. Rose Alban took a moment to wrap her fingers around the white steel balcony railing right in front of her, and squeeze. Gorgeous men were *not* allowed in her home, and her friend Tana knew that. Twenty-plus years of friendship down the drain, just like that. Too bad.

Pascal Cortes alighted from the ride-share sedan, wheeling a single silver hard-case luggage, the kind that would fit in the overhead compartment on a plane. Was he always this tall? Might have been twenty years since she last saw him—and he would have been nineteen. Did people grow taller like that in their twenties and thirties? Didn't nineteen-year-olds already have their adult faces? Why could she barely recognize this man?

Might have been her eyes. Rose did need to rest her eyes after several hours of screen time. Except it was a beautiful morning, a clear day, and she had been awake barely thirty minutes, and hadn't at all used a phone or another device. She might be forty-one but her eyes were not playing tricks on her.

He stopped in front of her home's gate. Barely a gate; a white fence really, that only came up to his thighs. Villa Dorothea Subdivision might be gated, but past the guardhouse, most homes inside were barely closed off. There was a homeowner's association rule against it. Fortresses were not part of the US suburbia aesthetic it had originally been based on. Pascal paused, and Rose could see him look at the little house-shaped attachment at the end of the gate, where the doorbell was. But he did not use it. Instead he reached for the latch and let himself in.

Well. That was presumptuous of him, wasn't it? How did he even know—? And then in an instant it was like Rose was twenty-one again, and she was at this very spot, watching as younger Pascal pulled over in his car, to pick up Tana whenever she'd hang out at the Alban home. Rose and Tana would be in the living room or the front porch, and he would eventually just let himself in. Exactly like that, by reaching over for the latch. He did not have to park and come in, but Tana told her that he liked when Rose's mom offered him something to eat. Rose's mom barely cooked—anything she offered would have been basic, or store-bought. Tana said it didn't matter, Pascal was a teenager, and would not pass up a chance to get food he didn't have to make or pay for.

Rose put her feet back in her slippers and reached for her phone. What was Pascal up to now, again? When Tana said her brother needed a place to stay in this part of the metro just for a few weeks, she was imagining a floppy-haired management student in cargo shorts. A quick search —one she should have done way before this moment—

informed her that she had missed a decade or two worth of memos. He was now Professor Pascal Cortes, MBA, head of operations of some startup called Pisara Education Tech. And he looked like *that.*

Why wouldn't he be all of this and more? Rose was definitely not doing the same things from twenty years ago. People had the right to change, and use all that time to do so.

Pascal not only led himself in through the gate, he also started wheeling his luggage in, self-assured. Like he knew the place very well, knew where to go. Well, he would be *wrong* about that, if he was going by memories from that long ago, because the Alban house in Villa Dorothea had changed since then. The garage that used to fit two cars had been converted into a studio apartment, detached from the main home and with its own entry point. If Pascal was thinking of going through the car park into the kitchen as he used to, he'd have a surprise obstacle in his way.

Which was why Rose would have to meet him downstairs, to let him in properly. Right. She *was* supposed to be his landlord, for the next five weeks.

THE OTHER THING that was different about the house now was that Rose was the only person who lived in it. Two floors, four rooms, a large kitchen, and the general energy and chaos of a set of parents and their three daughters. They moved into that house when Rose, the eldest, was nine years old, and it had been the first room she had all to herself. It felt like a luxury at that age to have her own space when she used to share one.

Then came the papers—US immigration papers to be

specific. That meant the Albans joined the ranks of Filipino families who packed their belongings and moved to another country. Husband and wife Joseph and Ramona, daughters Annika and Carly.

Not Rose. Rose was twenty-three when the approval came in, and because she was no longer a minor, had "aged out" of the process. It was a petition for immigration that had been filed on the year she was born, and only got approved when she was old enough to be excluded from it. Did that make any sense at all? No, but there were many like her. They had since changed the law to keep this from happening, but that change didn't apply to her. So she was one of many "aged out" eldest children, who found themselves suddenly separated from their families via immigration. Aged-out people who were suddenly independent twenty-somethings in charge of family homes, elderly relatives, and other adult matters. It was a thing! Rose was by no means the only one.

At the time, it didn't feel like family separation; she was a few years out of college, and her career was taking off. Her friends were stressing out over whether they could afford to move out, and here she was, experiencing it in reverse. *She* got to "move out" but stay exactly in the same place, have most of her support system intact. What she had to get used to was an emptier house.

It felt large and empty now, since she was rushing to get downstairs. From the balcony she had to go through her bedroom, then the hallway, then the stairs that led into the living room, then go past the dining room into the kitchen, and then finally, go out the door that used to lead to the garage. Now it just led out into the small alley that separated the house from the studio apartment that they built over the garage space.

Pascal was in front of the studio's door. But he was also looking up, no doubt wondering what this thing was doing there.

"Pascal," she said. "You're early."

"When did this happen?"

Something jumped in Rose's chest at the sound of his voice. She hadn't expected him to sound so—so handsome. Yes, people sounded attractive, that was a thing she was into, okay? It had been way too long and maybe she'd never really talked to him, so she didn't know what he would sound like. His voice sounded like it would make her feel warm if it wrapped around her. Like it would feel like it would tickle her skin.

"When did what happen?"

"No space for the cars anymore?"

Rose shrugged. "No more cars. You know the entire family moved away right? When Tana told you that I was renting out a space, where did you think you'd stay?"

Pascal grinned, and there was that younger version of him again. Still there, despite the serious suit. "I thought I'd stay in the house with you. It's a large house." That smile—like he was on campus, being flirty, being that guy everyone wanted to be friends with, wanted to date. And he did date a lot through the years, if Rose remembered Tana's stories right.

"*No*," she said, pointing to the studio. "You're staying here."

"There's no nostalgia in this. I don't recognize it. Does it even have a kitchen?"

"It has a kitchenette! A microwave. A mini refrigerator. You won't starve."

"But I love your kitchen." Seriously, a thirty-nine year

old man was pouting right there on her premises. "I thought I'd be seeing it again."

Yes it was a nice kitchen, but it had been modified and redecorated to suit Rose and her actual use of it. It was on one hand comforting to hear someone have good feelings toward the house. On the other hand, that actual space didn't exist as it used to anymore.

"You can have breakfast in there," Rose offered. After saying it she thought it was actually quite generous, and not an inconvenience for her; she usually did make breakfast, so doubling the serving wouldn't be so hard. Plus he was paying for his stay. This was fine.

"Awesome," Pascal said, and it seemed like he really did want it. "I'll tell you what I like for breakfast."

"No, you'll eat what I serve you."

"Wow, the hospitality at this place needs work."

Rose laughed. "I was about to make breakfast right now. Let's put your stuff in the studio and you can complain about my hospitality in the house."

2

Of course, Rose Alban had always been stunning. Her being two years older didn't seem like a problem now but back then, it was like the most impossible gap to leap over. He was too bookish, too awkward, still in school. She'd *never* be into a guy like him. Also, she was his older sister's friend and he was barely there to them, even when he was in the same house, or the same car.

One time, back then, Pascal Cortes allowed himself to think about Rose *that way* and decided he shouldn't. The few times they'd interacted, she'd talk about beautiful things she liked that he knew nothing about—boutique hotels, bed and breakfasts, pastries, clothes. He...was a college guy. He felt entirely uninteresting.

And he kept going to school for a long time after, getting his master's degree, then his MBA, then consulting for the education division of a multilateral, then teaching at business school.

All accomplishments his parents would obnoxiously bring up at reunions sure, but Rose had worked in political and social development communications for years. These were standard qualifications for every other person she'd met; she wouldn't have been impressed.

Easy as that, she was out of his league, and it seemed like she would always be.

And yet here they were. Now almost, kind-of, possible. The crackling certainty that the woman in front of him was *still* sexy and desirable in every way he liked. This year, of all years.

Pascal had declared to everyone and his sister that this was going to be the year he Stopped Fucking Around and for the most part, he was doing well. He'd left full-time teaching and had just started as head of operations of Pisara Education Tech, a new company founded by some friends and former business school contacts. They were all about the tech part, so he was actually (finally) sought and valued for the education part.

It was a drastic career change, but he was...doing okay? Pascal was actually caring about work again, and was even on top of his own laundry and bills. He hadn't even gotten a lecture from Tana about anything for *weeks*; he considered that progress. If he was being evaluated on acting like an actual adult, he might even be somewhat satisfactory.

It had been Tana's idea that he stay at Rose's while the new office was being prepped to open and of course, he said yes. He'd only need to walk, and he knew the family from before and felt welcome in the house. The rent was a miracle for the neighborhood it was in, a "friendly" rate that let everyone save face and ensured his stay wouldn't be an inconvenience or financial burden.

Pascal didn't realize that Rose lived there. By herself.

His sister set him up.

"When did the remodeling happen?" Pascal helped

himself to the usual spot where he used to sit, there at the center island, where Mrs. Alban would serve him a sandwich. But the chair was different, and so was the countertop, and yeah there was that matter of the garage being completely gone and a studio apartment being there in its place.

Rose was looking at him funny, as she made a few trips from the refrigerator to the stove. Did she think he wouldn't notice the changes? She had a great house, and he remembered thinking he wanted one just like it "when he grew up." Pascal's family had been on the lower end of the upper middle class; owned their home but didn't get to have a second floor. This house had that and a lawn and everything, something that imprinted on Pascal as a teen wandering through the halls on the way to the bathroom.

"It's been a work in progress for over a decade," she said. "Always sprucing it up, in case I needed to sell it."

"And you haven't been able to? Or you don't need to sell it."

"Not right now."

Pascal would buy it if he could. But too late, he already made too many choices that kept him hovering several income brackets away from affording this. "But you get income from renting the studio out?"

"Not so much, because I'm very picky. It's not listed on the usual sites. They need to be true friends of true friends."

"Why wouldn't you want to—"

"It's not safe." The stove was facing the north window, and to look at him, Rose would have to turn her back on it. She was holding a sandok, and oil was crackling behind her, and the smell of garlic slowly filled the air. "It's just me in here, and I refuse to get a manager for that tiny property outside, and it's not safe to have a steady stream of strangers coming in. The neighborhood association won't allow that either."

She was right, and Pascal bit his tongue to stop suggesting things.

She was still looking at him. "What?"

"What?"

"What do you think I should be doing instead, Professor Cortes?"

"I'm not a *full* professor," he muttered, but she wasn't going to be interested in that story. "And I'm not going to presume to know better than you when it comes to this house and your finances. I haven't even been here an hour."

"Good answer."

"By the end of week two, watch out."

Rose laughed, and turned back to the stove. She peeled the lid off a reusable container and dumped cold rice into her pan, joining the oil and the garlic.

Oh God, she was making sinangag.

Did Tana know—his sister was pure evil. Even worse, Rose made eggs, sunny side up. Sprinkled some chili flakes on them. Popped some longganisa into the microwave. Soon, the kitchen, though remodeled and on the surface unfamiliar, warmed up into the welcoming space he used to know, used to enjoy hanging out in for a few minutes before his sister was ready to go, and he drove them back home. Garlic and rice—that was part of the character of the house apparently, and he didn't notice until now.

This was a lot of things he liked.

No, don't think about that.

He didn't have to feel anything. He was practically a stranger to Rose, and she absolutely did not look like a goddess in what might have been the shorts and shirt she slept in, hair up in a bun, cooking breakfast. Never had he wanted anything so...domestic. His fantasies were set in every place other than this.

Free food. These feelings were in anticipation of free food.

Maybe it was safer if he just went back home.

Why did you let me rent the studio for that cheap? Pascal practiced that in his head, already formulating some kind of exit strategy. Maybe there was a waiting list and better paying renters ready to swoop in. Maybe it would be better for her if he backed out now, and he wouldn't have to worry about what it meant that he was ogling her as she made him something to eat.

"How's your mom?" Pascal asked. Best way to kill inappropriate thoughts.

Rose looked at him funny again, but then answered anyway. "Great, actually. Looking at retirement options."

"Not coming back here?"

"It's too soon." Rose thought about it and giggled. "It's weird how twenty years is 'too soon,' but for them it is so they're not coming back just yet. But they are going to need the extra income, so thank you for renting the studio."

"It's way below market rental price. I should be thanking you."

"I did it for Tana. And she promised me you would deep clean that thing before you leave."

How many times did his sister set him up in one transaction? She was unbelievable. And yet, he couldn't work himself up to real anger, because the breakfast he was about to get smelled great.

"Are they visiting anytime soon?"

"My parents?" Rose shrugged. "I don't think so. They never really come over in June. Summer over there is great for them."

"I'm glad they're doing great." Pascal was sincere about that. "Dad had a minor heart attack but he's okay."

"Thank God. Isn't it awful that this is what we talk about?"

On this, the year that he Stopped Fucking Around, Pascal actually did come to terms with the fact that he *was* at that age, and that these conversations were standard. From never mentioning his parents in casual conversation, now their health was the first topic of practically every single one. It was a shared experience, yep, of people of a certain age. Sobering but helpful. Its own kind of support group.

"So wait—you used to work with Tana, right?" Pascal asked. "But you left political comms work. Or she left first, I'm not sure what happened."

"*She* left first, to get her masters. I tried to stick around in the industry for a few years."

"Did you go back to school too?"

"No, God." She said it with a mirthful laugh. "Not everyone likes to collect degrees like you and Tana do."

He couldn't defend that, and didn't. And as if that wasn't enough, this career shift was like school all over again. "And is being manager of family affairs taking up all of your time?"

It was cute but disarming, the way her face instantly armored up with wary skepticism. She set a yellow plate in front of him and told him to serve himself. Cool, because this *wasn't* so domestic. She really was just treating him like a chore, and this wasn't anything special, and he would be out of her mind as soon as he was out of her sight.

When he headed over to the stove where the rice and longganisas were—it was another trap. She'd made a large serving, and he didn't know how much he should serve himself. A lot would be too eager, wouldn't it? But she'd have to know that this was what he did, in the Alban house. In their kitchen. A small serving would seem like he was just going through the motions, that he didn't want this. It would also be a lie because he wanted all of this in his mouth.

He went for authenticity.

"Hungry?" She teased him. Her own serving was probably a fourth of his, and she finished up quickly. "Wash your own dishes when you're done," she told him, before she left him in the kitchen. "And there's a copy of my contact info on a card in the studio, in case you need anything."

That was it—landlord/hospitality manager stuff over. Rose waved at him and disappeared further into the house and after a while, he couldn't even hear her footsteps. Pascal could enjoy this meal on his own. In theory, it should give him the same satisfaction even if she weren't there.

The food was excellent. Kitchen seemed nice but also quiet now.

Pascal looked up rental rates in the area again and true enough, everything else was damn expensive. And more so because he was looking for something on short notice. It wasn't a good idea to "check out" of here now. He did need to make it to the office early in the morning every day and close it up late at night. He didn't need the unnecessary travel and appreciated sleep at his age.

Whatever, he had already packed his luggage, was already here. For Pascal, work and school and teaching *always* came first, and he was clear about it. That focus never wavered, even when he was dating someone, and he tried to tell them that no matter how good it got between them, his priorities would remain the way they were.

Obviously this caused problems in the past, and was the

reason why he was single, and why anyone who cared about their friends never set them up with him.

He wouldn't even need to *see* Rose. Big house, detached studio. These next five weeks would go by so quickly he wouldn't even notice.

3

"You okay with the front lawn?"

"But it's *hot*, Rose. Or it might rain."

"We can do the shoot in the living room but only as plan Z or something."

"Of course because by then we'll need a roof or air-conditioning. Why isn't the teeny apartment available?"

Rose was hoping she could go all five weeks without telling Ana Bellina Cuadrado, her best friend and business partner at Zora/Maya, that she had a hot professor living in her studio apartment. Did not expect to have to cave on day one. Not that Bels would have a problem with the concept. It was that she would be too excited, and if she saw what Pascal looked like, she would start *planning* very embarrassing things.

Because while Rose was perfectly fine in her house, working on their small and specific fashion business from the office that used to be her childhood bedroom, and doing the required regular photo shoots in the studio apartment, Bels suddenly became the one who insisted on going everywhere, meeting everyone, doing everything. They didn't start out this way because Rose wouldn't even have thought of starting this new phase of her career with someone so *bubbly*. As Bels got older, she seemed to get out of her shell more. Rose was on a different personal journey and happened to like her shell.

"You mean *this guy? Is living in the studio right now?*" Bels thrust the phone into Rose's face. When Rose's vision cleared, she was confronted with a photo of Pascal sitting on a freaking fence and smiling at someone just off camera. What the hell—? She had read that article, yes. That was how she found out about Pascal's achievements, his current career move. What she didn't see was the six-slide fashion editorial style photo shoot that accompanied the article. Was that how they covered education tech startups now?

The styling, the cozy rumpling of him, the "shucks I have several degrees and care about education"—it was exactly the reformed and revived Pascal of her lust-filled imagination. That her friend Bels, a person she trusted a lot in terms of judgment and taste, was validating that the man was hot meant...it wasn't an illusion. It wasn't her hormones acting up. It wasn't her usually alone in this big house suddenly being not so alone in the big house.

Hot sexy man really was just a few steps and a knock away.

"This is *interesting.* And you know him? You're friends with—?"

"His sister."

"This is Tana Cortes's *brother*? He didn't look like this before!"

"Of course he did, I just—" Rose just didn't care. "He was nineteen."

Bels laughed. "Yuck. Okay, I get it. But he would be thirty-eight or thirty-nine now. *Interesting.*"

Rose missed Single Bels. Her friend had been the exact same person but she never suggested anyone for Rose to date. Instead her suggestions were usually about cake, cocktails, or a new vacation destination to try.

"You're *not* interested in this?" The phone with its photographic evidence was again in Rose's face. "Wait. Do we hate his political choices?"

Rose sighed. "We do not." It was one thing she found in her Google search—he was very vocal in his support of human rights and equality and instantly became ten times more attractive.

"So what's wrong? Is it a past relationship? Why is he single at thirty-nine? Anything in his past? You can find out easily, right?" Then her friend's face changed. "You know what, never mind that. Unmarried by choice at our age is just how it is."

"Thank you," Rose said. "And I can always ask Tana if there's anything to be warned about. Not for anything else. Just general safety."

"A blessing." Bels looked at the photo on her phone one last time before shrugging and putting it away. "But you know I'm just having fun with you, right? Nothing has to happen really. I mean, we have a lot going on. You have a lot going on. He can just be a guy who stays in the studio. Nothing has to happen."

"That's *nice* of you to say, Bels. I miss the days when you didn't care whether I dated or not."

"Is it that bad now?" She blinked. "I'm sorry. Yuck, have I become that friend?"

"I'm guessing you're in a good place and that's fine. Just reminding you that that's your business."

"Noted." Bels peeked at her phone again. "Professor Cortes has some nice arms though."

Bels was happily dating a guy from the national hockey team, and truth be told, Rose was surprised that they were getting along. He didn't seem to be her type. But maybe that was the point, and the reason, for it. They seemed to have taken it slow, didn't do labels, dated when they felt like it, gave it time, and thought things through.

Rose may be horny as per usual but she also knew she didn't care for the theatrics anymore. So many things about relationships were exhausting and frankly, she didn't have any energy to spare. Work was enough. Managing her family's everything was taking up what was left. If she had any sliver of strength left, it would be going to making herself a good meal and enjoying it. She liked her routine and her life as is.

Nothing had to happen, Rose.

4

Six hours of his life gained back (per day!), by choosing to rent a place closer to the office. That was a good deal. Pascal was needed there in the morning, because he wanted to see how the interiors of the conference rooms were coming along, and again in the early evening when the last of the new staff training ended. In between, he still needed to work, or sleep, but he couldn't do that from the site yet. Six 32 Central was one of those black holes in the city that he could end up trapped in if he didn't plan his day well. It could spit him out early but then he wouldn't be able to make it back for the early evening closing. Or he'd need to stay there until late and then be a zombie at the site the next morning.

"...and that's the end of module 2. I'd like everyone to do the test from their phones this time, using mobile data. Did the connection in room 5 work?"

It still hadn't, which was a problem. Pascal added it to the list of things that couldn't yet be checked off. He waited as everyone who'd come to the morning training packed up and left, and went back to the ongoing video call he had with the people who were technically his bosses, siblings Leandro and Daniella Alano, founders of Pisara Education Tech. Their new venture was providing all these new and tech-enhanced ways to help teachers and learners; Pascal was brought in as the education person, Leandro was on top of tech, Daniella handled the money. They were not at the office with him though. Leandro preferred to work from the beach, and Daniella was in Hong Kong. Pascal did not envy these choices. It would annoy him to interrupt actual fun with a work call. Some people's lives were work—he was glad he could walk away from an actual office at the end of the day.

It was *cool*, by the way, to live and work within a fifteen-minute walk again. That it was even possible. He was done with his first meeting before noon, and then wondered what to do with all the time. Maybe he could explore what was about to be his work neighborhood, where he'd have coffee, where he'd invite people to out-of-office meetings. He walked by a chicken sandwich takeout place, ordered one, and decided to walk back home.

Rose Alban's home, was his quick mental correction. The Alban household. That he was a temporary tenant of. When he turned the corner into the familiar street in Villa Dorotea Subdivision, it struck him suddenly what he had earned back by making this choice to live here for now. He'd have time—time to work, time to sleep, time to do absolutely nothing.

Pascal congratulated himself on this. Sometimes he did not screw things up.

The sound of the gate was not what it used to be. It was squeakier before, heavier in his hand somehow. The changes to the house included repainting the gate and greasing its hinges. Rose's mom used to say she knew it was him from how he let the latch fall, and it must have been that loud. He was graceless at that age. Arguably graceless to this day. At least the gate showed some character development.

He could see from the big windows that looked into the living room that Rose had a guest. He thought she would be out for some reason, on a Friday at noon, but no. He tried to remember now what Tana said she was up to. A fashion business. Possibly run from home?

His sister Tana had worked with Rose in the early days of their career in political communications. Then politics became unbearable for both of them. Tana worked in non-political PR for a while but had since returned to David Alano's comm staff. Rose had apparently left that world entirely and started her own business.

Pascal wasn't thinking. He just walked into the front door like he was still a teen and it was fine to do that.

"Hello there!" Rose's guest said. Around the same age as Rose, but smiling a lot wider. "I'm Ana. Bellina. Cuadrado. Rose's business partner and best friend ever. But you can call me Bels. You're her new tenant!"

"Yes I am," he said. "Pascal Cortes."

"Tana's brother," Rose added. "Not some dude traveler off the internet."

"Was that a concern?" Pascal asked. "Yes I'm actually familiar with the place. Had merienda here all the time, right in this kitchen."

"So how was your first night in the studio?" Bels said, cheerily like a hotel concierge.

"Five stars," he said. "Would recommend to other non-strangers."

Rose laughed but didn't say anything, and instead turned her back to them, attention on a pile of fabric on the table. Bels was still looking at him with bright, wide eyes.

"I'm glad I got to meet you, because it's good to vet the tenants somehow some way, right? For Rose's own security. Will you be throwing any loud parties while you're staying here, Mr. Cortes? Inviting any loud companions?"

Rose might not be looking but for sure everyone was listening, so Pascal said it anyway. "No loud parties or loud companions. Not this year. Not anymore."

"Oh. You're at *that* phase of life, it's very familiar. Forty?"

"Thirty-nine."

"Welcome to this side of the divide, Pascal. I'm really truly kidding about the loud parties and companions. It's just good to know that my best friend Rose doesn't have to be worried about her tenant."

"Oh, the loud parties thing is a valid concern," Rose interrupted, still not even looking at them. "I can't get in trouble with the neighborhood association here. They're already allowing me to offer temporary leases under very specific conditions. One of them is noise level." *Then* she chose to turn and look at him. "Just make sure your companions are quiet, Pascal."

He wasn't even thinking of bringing anyone over but yeah some people might think—"I'm not going to get you in any kind of trouble."

Bels's gaze bounced between both of them, and then she clasped her hands. Still cheery as a tourism representative. "Well. It's great that we met. Now that I see you I realize you could help us out."

"Us?" Rose protested. "With what?"

"With our *collection*. That we are *working on right now.*" Bels cleared her throat. "I'm not sure you're familiar with Zora/Maya, Pascal. It's our small but growing business that is specifically about rethinking corporate and academic style. Business wear and uniforms. For this climate. Using sustainable and local fabrics. Produced in ethical ways. Named after our maternal grandmothers. Maybe you can help us out?"

"Sure, with what? It's been a while since I consulted for fashion or retail, but do you need something for your business plan? Supply chain? Capitalization?"

Bels laughed. "Oh, not that. We've got all of that covered. We would like you to *model*. Our clothes. Would you be able to do that?"

5

Well that wasn't awkward at *all.*

For the record, it wasn't like Rose was completely new at this game. Their business was small but they were "buzzy," their website was shiny, and the photographs were always gorgeous. As much as possible, they asked people who would really wear their clothes in real life to model for them but they still needed people who would photograph well, so she had been in the presence of hot models. Often. A *gazillion* times.

Still, the idea that Pascal Cortes would be the subject of a shoot and she would have to dress him in the near future...made her feel something.

It was logical. He would look good in the short-sleeved Clasico button-down. If he wore a white shirt under the chocolate blazer...the thought of it made Rose's knees weak. It was embarrassing.

Right after saying yes to modeling, he excused himself to head back to the studio apartment. Rose and Bels went back to their test shoot for the new sample pouches, and didn't see him again for the rest of the day.

As night began to fall, she didn't see him either, and that made sense. It was a Friday night, and her house was a quick walk from a district where one could actually have a social life. The business district's expansion was creeping toward residential subdivision Villa Dorotea. In another three years Rose would probably hear club noises in her bedroom. How would that make her feel? As it was, everyone out in the bars and clubs looked so young, so into other things.

No they're not young. Not necessarily. Every time she tried to date, she met another person forty and up who had made similar choices as she did, or was looking to start anew. With that out of the way, the problem finally revealed itself. *You just don't like any of them.*

On Fridays, Bels and Rose worked a nearly full day. Then Bels would take off and nowadays probably see the hockey guy, so Rose had her own Friday ritual. She'd make a quick dinner in a bowl, mix a cocktail she'd looked up online, and bring both upstairs to her favorite place in the entire house—her bedroom's balcony.

And she would change into not-work clothes. She actually *would* wear Zora/Maya as she worked, so when she switched from that mode to weekend, it was comfortable pants and tank top time.

Mom: Missed video call
Mom: Missed video call
Mom: Did you tell Teresa you're bringing a plus one?

At least it wasn't a voice call. Unplanned voice calls were *not* good, as far as her family was concerned.

Video calls, on the other hand, were fine. That was just Mom saying hi, first thing in the morning (for her). And then the follow-up chat message indeed reinforced how it was just Mom being Mom.

Should she reply now, or later? But if she didn't do it now, Mom might try to call her again. And that would be a longer conversation.

Rose: It's just a despedida, right? Why am I bringing a plus one?

Teresa was her twenty-something cousin who was about to relocate to...Canada? To be honest Rose had forgotten when this was going to be, and where Teresa was moving exactly, and what was the reason again. These despedidas blended into each other, or maybe she actually thought Teresa had already left. Her family wasn't unusual in that way, she was sure; someone was always coming and going. Despedida dinner here, balikbayan lunch there.

As the only family member in town she was supposed to represent everyone, and drop off the family gift as needed.

Mom: There's a sit-down dinner so they want to know how many seats.
Rose: One?
Mom: So there's no one worth bringing?
Rose: To Teresa's despedida? Nah.
Mom: I'll tell them. So still single?
Mom: Can we talk about the petition then?

Oh for the love of—there really was no winning this one. In Rose's case, being single was not a misery scenario for her family, because it meant something else. Rose remaining single at her age, still, meant she would likely be eligible for that immigration petition they had filed on her behalf.

Rose: I'm going to read the stuff soon.
Mom: You said that last year.

Was it that long ago already? Rose knew there was a regular calendar update for the priority date but she hadn't looked at it in a while. Or at all. One of the upsides of this cross-ocean family circumstance was she could say she was going to look at it...and then not do that.

Rose: I will do that really! Anyway it's late and I'm going to bed now.
Mom: It's not late.
Rose: I worked all day! Good night, love you.

Rose left her phone in her bedroom when she stepped back out onto the balcony to enjoy her Friday night.

WHEN PEOPLE FOUND out why Rose was living in a big house by herself, they often made a face, and a sound, like they'd heard a Sad Thing. Poor Rose, a victim of wonky immigration policy, missed out on the "golden ticket" that her entire family got, to live in the "first world."

It did suck, the separation and almost arbitrary denial of something her parents and two sisters were given.

But also: eighteen years did not go by in a regretful blur. Rose enjoyed many of those years, a lot. Sometimes she didn't admit this because it felt disrespectful to do so, but the same privilege that made her family's move a sure thing also made things easier for her once they left. You'd never catch her complaining. Her family moved out but she was able to settle into what they had built.

Settling, whenever Rose heard it to refer to her situation, did not sting at all. Settling reminded her of her favorite chair, this balcony, this bedroom—the master bedroom, which she had moved into—and this house. It reminded her that she had a place, and as this new career and young business was taking off, that having roots wasn't holding her back. For years people told her that the house was a burden, that it needed to be dumped so she could be free. In the past decade or so she'd transformed it into a workspace, a rental, and something she could call hers.

Constantly questioning this was making her more protective of it. Rose was trying to outgrow that reflex, honestly. Because what if they had a point? What if this wasn't where she was supposed to be, and she had *contraried* herself to a lesser life?

The drink she had tried to make tonight was a cucumber melon soju, paired with fried chicken in a bowl of rice, and this wasn't too bad at all. This was what she wanted to do tonight.

"Oh shit." The surprised voice came from just below her, where someone at the door of the studio apartment would be. "You're up there."

It could only be Pascal so thank goodness it actually was. Pascal looked like he just came back from work.

"You're early," Rose said.

"It's almost ten."

"Yeah, but it's Friday. Unless you're heading out again?"

"I'm tired, Rose."

She burst out laughing.

At night, she kept the driveway lights on until she went

to bed and then the motion sensors kicked in. The effect was what was practically a spotlight on his big, sturdy frame, his handsome face. He did look like the walk was warmer than he'd planned; there was a sheen of sweat on his forehead. And she was looking down toward him like some hacienda mistress. This was absurd.

"Want something to eat?"

6

"But—" Rose was shaking her head, her laugh practically bubbling into her drink. "But you were putting in the time."

"I *know* right." He promised himself just this week that he would stop whining about jobs and ranks he didn't get, but here he was two drinks down and telling the entire story all over again to a willing ear. *For the last time, Pascal.* "I would have gotten the better offer if I worked overseas, but not if I helped put the program together here. Which I did."

"It doesn't make sense. Ugh, I don't miss organizational politics at all. So you just started your own company then?"

"I didn't start it, but David's cousins did, and they need someone with my experience. And I know Leandro and Daniella from grad school anyway." David Alano, Philippine senator, and his sister's significant other. Pascal had maybe whined to David about the job he was never going to get, and David's idea that he consider joining the new venture offered a stepping stone, but also an out. So the next stage of Pascal's career began. It wasn't where he thought he would be as he turned forty—he thought he would be promoted and settled in, not starting over.

"Wasn't this your parents' room?" he asked.

Rose laughed. "Yes, but I'm the queen of this castle now, so I get the largest bedroom." She added, "And it was part of the deal, when I agreed to stay in the house once they left. It had to be mine. It took some work but the title's in my name now. I can't be made to live here and they still make the decisions about the property from another country. I'm not a guest here—I *own* it. When they visit, they're the guests."

"Showing them who's boss."

"Exactly."

It was a great house, and even though he had never been to this part of it, it did feel like hers now. Well, he tried not to look at the bedroom too much when he walked past it. The balcony he'd seen from outside, and now that he was hanging out on it with her, felt keenly how it was her space. She had a lounge chair even, and a small table that held their food and drinks beside it. He was sitting on a cushioned rattan chair they'd pulled out from inside the bedroom, not as loungey but still very comfortable. The balcony was facing the subdivision and not the sprawling business district right behind it. Up here it still looked like it was quiet out there.

If he had taken up any of his friends' offers to hang out at a bar on the walk home, he would have missed this.

Pascal raised his glass to her. "And I'm guessing the home improvements were yours? Since you took over ownership?"

"Thanks." She toasted, looking pleased. "Yes. I know some of them are drastic from back when you last saw it, but I had to make it work for me. It's not going to be a house for a couple and three kids."

"Never?"

Rose shook her head. "Not the plan. But it is a lot of space so it's a home office, a studio, a meeting area. It's close enough to many workplaces so we get to go on our meetings without going too far. And most of our clients are in the city just over there."

"Genius."

"It's lemonade. The kind I had to learn to make because suddenly the four other people who lived here moved out. But that's the summary of my life since you were last here. It's all lemonade."

When she took a long drink from her glass of soju—not lemonade—Pascal felt it. Felt the years and compromises behind that short statement.

"You don't need me to say it, but it all looks great," Pascal said. "It's yours. Formed it into something that you would find functional. I didn't do that I guess, and that was my mistake, wasn't it? I really thought if I worked long enough and put in the face time, they'd have no choice but to give the job to me."

Her smile was small, sympathetic. "Oh, we can't ever assume we will be given things, even the things we thought we earned, Pascal."

"I know that now, haha." He drank to that. "Is this what conversations are like now? How are your parents, these are my regrets?"

Rose visibly shuddered. "You tried dating people, right? It's either useless small talk, or no talking at all."

"No talk because—?"

"All sex. Yeah that's what I meant." She shrugged. "But no talking isn't so bad sometimes."

For a moment, right when Pascal met her eyes and realized he had no ready response, all he did was feel what it probably meant. Recalculate Rose with the new information that she might want—no talking.

Her eyelashes fluttered. "Small talk is the worst. Are you seeing anyone now, Pascal?"

"Did my sister tell you anything about me?"

"Not lately, sorry. I didn't even know you were teaching at the business school."

Great, his own sister wasn't talking him up, but whatever. "I dated, not serious with anyone for years now, but I also declared to her that this year, I was not going to fuck up."

"And that means what?"

"It means I tend to ruin relationships in general so if I don't want to fuck up at all, I shouldn't even date."

"That's hilarious."

"It's the responsible thing to do."

"Like a relationship doesn't take two. Like all you need to do is back off and things will be fine. Like the other party doesn't have just as much right and opportunity to walk away."

Well when she said it that way...of course it took two. "I'm doing my part by not initiating."

As if he hadn't just come up to her bedroom, didn't just spend more than an hour now talking about his life and hers, didn't just choose to spend Friday night on this balcony enjoying her homemade cocktails instead of drinks poured for him at any establishment on the same block as his new office. He made a *bunch* of choices that might be construed as initiating.

Rose stretched ever so slightly, the motion pushing herself up and back into the recliner. It did something to her hair, changed the way it fell on her shoulders and framed her face, made her look like she was in bed, looking at him that way. Of course it was sexy; this entire conversation he'd been trying not to look at her too much, and failing mostly.

"In that case," Rose said, "that's great and maybe I should thank you for one less toxic relationship in the world."

"You're welcome." He was usually prouder of this resolution to proactively preempt douche behavior. This time, he was kind of apologetic. It was a strange feeling, or maybe it was the soju.

"Help me bring these back to the kitchen?"

And just like that, this was over, and he was being dismissed. Maybe it would be the last time he'd be invited up to her tower, and he'd deserve it. At least he and Rose had caught up, and he learned that he could still hold a conversation that might interest her, and she was fine without any further participation by him in her life.

Dishes and glasses were left in the sink in the kitchen, but she walked with him to the door and until he was right outside the studio apartment.

"I have to check the gate. You should go in," Rose told him.

It was after midnight. He had nowhere else to go and nothing else to do, but the feeling that he wanted to do *something* gnawed at him. He wanted to be somewhere other than the door to his new temporary place. He didn't want to be saying good night.

"Thanks for dinner," Pascal said, coming closer for a tentative half hug. Seemed like the thing to do, something probably acceptable now that they were older. He'd never gotten to that level of close back then, didn't even try. Tonight, he attempted the half hug, one arm circling her back, cheeks touching for a whisper of a second. No big deal.

Someone miscalculated, someone overstepped. Not him, he was sure of it. Regardless, in the next beat, instead of cheeks touching, it was the corner of his mouth brushing against the corner of hers. So quick, and also, so close. A current ran through both of them, the effect being a mutual gotcha, like a thing had been peeled away.

Someone did it first and he wasn't sure who, but her lips were on his, or his lips were on hers. Soft lips and gentle breathing. Pascal didn't even remember when he'd last kissed anyone in a way that lingered. Sweet and soft.

Rose pulled away first, touching her lips. A bit of "what the hell had just happened" in her eyes. "Um. Thanks. Good night?"

"Rose—"

"It's okay. That was nice. I just don't think it's a good idea to, well...you don't get sex with the rent. It's weird. Also you're not paying enough. Okay, that sounded even weirder. It's just better if it's not on the table for us, if you're living here. I hope you understand. And I do actually respect your mission to not fuck up. You should stay on that path. Good night."

Well there was nothing more to say to that, was there? He was dismissed. "Yes, good night. That was—thank you."

"You turned out okay, Pascal."

Oh no, that really was the ultimate kiss-off. "Thank you, Rose."

7

T*wo weeks later*

"Pascal?"

Rose's voice right then, along with the knocking on the studio door, wasn't the huge surprise it should have been. Maybe he'd caught himself imagining—hoping for—that sound combination, more than once. Anyway, it was real, and he had to pause a sec to make sure it was actually happening.

Pascal had kept away from her and the house for a while. Two weeks, to the day. It was Friday night again and he was just about to heat up his takeout dinner, and since it was really Rose out there, she would know and see that he was home and had no plans. For a second, he thought of what excuse would explain his lack of plans but then he scrapped it. It had been a long week, and he looked forward to staying in. That was it, no profound reason really.

It was seven-thirty, meaning he got home earlier than usual, and he had already showered and changed. Already settled in. He was thinking he'd be asleep by ten. If this made her even less impressed, then what was new. Why would it even matter?

"You're home, thank God!" When he opened the door to find her in a deep blue dress, her lips a dark plum color, and her mood slightly panicky, he got concerned. "Do you have plans tonight? Can I borrow you for a bit? You can start your binge watch in an hour, or two at most!"

Yeah his Netflix home screen was visible from here and he *was* about to start a season of whatever but he wasn't going to explain that anymore. "I don't mind. What's wrong?"

She stepped back and looked him up and down. "Nothing's wrong. I'm just—I just lied about something and now I need your help. Can you wear a shirt with a collar or something? Do you have one? Something with longer sleeves? Ugh I should have brought you something. Oh wait—" Rose walked right into his apartment—her apartment—and nudged open the drawer of the coffee table in front of his TV. Neatly folded men's shirts in blue and brown and purple were inside. "Good, I forgot to move these back into the house. Please change into this one?"

Rose was handing him a dark purple shirt, with the collar and sleeves that she was asking for. Pascal peeled off his Anselmo Graduate School blue and white round-neck right in front of her, and slid the new shirt over his head. It smelled faintly of floral fabric conditioner, and felt really comfortable on him. "Is this what you make? It's great."

"Oh, thank you. Um, pants too?"

The studio did not have a separate bedroom, and his jeans were on the bed. Anyway, he changed right there anyway, sort of angling to the side as he swapped his sweatpants for the jeans.

Rose had been looking away and greeted him with a sheepish smile when he was done. "So this is, um, dinner, and I don't have time to explain everything yet, so please just follow my lead okay?"

"What exactly is this thing?" After that (accidental) kiss and then two weeks of silence, this was out of the ordinary but he wasn't going to complain. Just asking questions. "I don't have my key—"

She was already locking the door, taking him by the hand and heading for the house. "It's fine, of course I have a key. I'll let you back in later. So this is dinner. With my mom and ten of her closest friends. And I just told them you're my fiancé. Follow my lead, okay?"

For the past two years, Pascal had been bitter about losing a role he had been extremely qualified for, to someone who was winging it. It didn't escape him that he was now in a role he didn't deserve, and was winging it. He had never been anyone's fiancé before. In the Philippines, land of no divorce, it was still expected to be a fiancé only once. There were no experts at it really, were there? Everyone had to be winging it.

Anyway, he hoped whatever he lacked in experience was being covered up nicely by smiling a lot, and being properly overwhelmed by Rose's big house now occupied by a lot of people. It also not-so-surprisingly only took the least adjustment to get comfortable looking at Rose like she was the most beautiful woman he'd ever seen. Not even acting.

At first he was worried that he'd say the wrong thing, but

Rose's mom's friends—the titas—spoke over each other all the freaking time. No story was told without interruption and at least three digressions until they'd forgotten that they were asking him something.

This wasn't so hard. He barely needed to do a thing.

Meanwhile, Rose touched his arm, or his elbow, one time took his hand right in full view of her mom, and then let go. He noticed that she was wearing an actual diamond ring, on her left ring finger.

"Your mom said you're still single!" one of the titas brazenly said to Rose, right in front him. "She was asking if I could introduce you to my daughter-in-law's cousin! Mona, I hope it's because you didn't know about Pascal, and not because you wanted someone else! He seems okay naman."

So this was happening right in front him, because titas were like that. Rose practically facepalmed. "No...I didn't tell my mom. Don't start chismis ha? I just wanted to keep this quiet because..."

"I understand, hija," another tita said, already speaking over Rose. "When you're over forty—and you are, right?—it's just better to not announce things until you're absolutely sure. It's humiliating when it doesn't work out, as you get older."

"Ha ha ha." Rose's smile was there but also stiff, stuck.

"So this means she's sure about this one now?" Another tita piped in. "You believe in whirlwind romances all of a sudden?"

"—It's not a whirlwind, is it? Don't you have common friends or something? Manila is such a small world you really will end up engaged to your childhood friend if you aren't married yet by forty—"

"—What are you even waiting for, hija? Why aren't you married now?"

"—hay naku even announcements aren't a sure thing, don't you remember Dolly's son, that was such a public engagement—"

"Didn't he go to *jail*?"

"No, that was Dolly's *brother*."

And then they were off on another set of conversations all together.

Pascal wasn't sure how his presence was making it better for her. If it wasn't well wishes coming in via backhands, it was direct hits. By a certain age, getting these digs from relatives was common, sure. He got them too. It was annoying but he also felt he had it coming. Rose, on the other hand, did not deserve any of this.

What he did next was a leap of faith that he knew he was taking, but he couldn't help it. He looped his arm around her waist, pulled her closer. It brought her head right under his chin, and he pressed a kiss on her hair. Rose put a hand on his knee and squeezed, gently, and then cuddled up closer. He did it to send a signal to the titas that he absolutely wasn't like Dolly's son, whatever that meant, but then this.

This was...it was fine.

If there was anyone who was not buying it, it was Rose's mom, Tita Ramona. She was looking at them like she was one of those profs who'd found a flaw in his paper, but wouldn't mention it right away, and instead bide their time.

Sometimes they did that. Ugh, the worst.

"You really didn't tell anybody you were flying in?" one of the titas was asking Tita Ramona, and Pascal trained his ear toward the answer. Yeah he did want to know too. He thought Rose wasn't expecting any visits from her family soon.

Tita Ramona turned toward her friend. "No, I didn't. It was a sudden thing. But we had miles and wanted to use it."

"Why didn't Jojo come along?"

"Ah, his brother is still recovering from surgery, he wanted to be there in case they needed an extra hand. You never know these days."

"And the girls are here too?"

"Yes, but they went out with their friends right away."

"Yeah, this is the Tita Zone," Rose said, disengaging from him to pick up an empty plate, and another.

"Lola Zone!" One of the titas joked. "I mean I'm sure you're giving your mom a grandkid soon, right? Even if you're over forty."

"Oh, no," Rose quickly answered. "No kids for me."

To the credit of some of the titas in the room, only half of them reacted like this was a disappointing thing to hear. That was some progress, and probably someone in their lives did the difficult work of breaking that convention. Still, half was ready to pounce with the questions.

"I don't want kids either," Pascal said. "So it works out for us."

He thought he said that to help, but he felt a distinctly sharp look from both Rose *and* her mother, identical almost, and whoops. Fine. He assumed he should go back to smiling and following her lead. Or better, helping her with the dishes, that she was now bringing into the kitchen from the family dining room.

"Am I doing okay?" he whispered, once he was right beside her by the sink. It felt like the titas would have heard anything above that decibel level. "Because your mom is really glaring at me. Reminds me of my worst profs."

Rose turned the water on, let the splashing sound on the dirty dishes cover their conversation. "Yeah, you're doing fine. I'm sorry I put you in this position, but it's fine, okay? And Mom will come around."

"Come around to what? To believing us or just not hating me?" He didn't want Tita Ramona to hate him. She was really nice to him back then. "I thought she would like the news that we're engaged."

"Are you *pouting?*"

"Why am I not good enough for her?"

Rose laughed, trying to keep it soundless. "The animosity you're sensing is not about you, it's about me completely lying to her about being in a relationship. After she asked me point blank recently if I had one."

"You're going to tell me about it, right? Why we had to do this."

"Of course," Rose said. "I'll tell you right now, since dinner's done. Let's get you out of here."

8

The front porch on an elevated wooden deck had always been there, but in recent years Rose had the steps and railings freshened up with paint and plants. It made the area another space that they could use as a photo shoot setting or backdrop.

Rose and Pascal could sit there by the railing and look into the window and see right through to the living room, where all the titas had moved. The titas could see outside too, and maybe from inside, it looked like Rose and Pascal were having a cozy moment, sitting together on the porch.

"That is fucked up," Pascal said, trying to keep his voice low.

"You never met anyone who aged out of a family petition before? It's really quite common. Or it was."

"I used to work with somebody, but she migrated maybe a year after I met her? She might have said this but I didn't think about what it meant. I didn't realize you had to stay unmarried while on petition. But yeah, she's a mom, was able to move to the US with her kid. Not with the kid's dad though."

"She was in her thirties?" Rose made a calculation, but knew what kind of visa it was. That was an accidental skill acquired from years of caring about this—she knew all the visa categories and their priority dates. "Same visa as mine likely. It'll cover her, and if she has a kid, but not the boyfriend. And if they married she'd have to change status."

"She loses her visa if she married the dad of her kid?"

"Well, they can just file her as married once one of her siblings becomes a citizen but that's a longer line. But people wait that long. My parents did."

Pascal was looking at her and whoa, how difficult and distracting it must have been to be his student in anything. "The wait is long enough that the eldest children get aged out of a petition. That's how your situation happened?"

"Yeah, but they made a bureaucratic fix for it, a few years after it happened to me. It probably doesn't happen as much anymore." Rose smiled at him. "I'm one of the last."

"That is fucked up."

"Look, I got a house, because my parents owned this. I'm aware some people who age out aren't as lucky. Sometimes it's the thing that derails their lives and they never recover. I saw how many times I could have screwed up here, but I got lucky. And I made lemonade." It was still funny when Rose tried to summarize almost twenty years in one go. So many things were going to sound uneventful out of context. No way to convey the highs and the lows.

He was shaking his head, now looking into the house, at the titas inside. As if they were responsible for her situation somehow, and there was some truth to that. "So it's the kind of system that separates families based on a backlog you had nothing to do with, and you're supposed to stay here and fend for yourself. You were practically a kid."

"I was twenty-three though." Technically not a minor

child, and she didn't feel like a kid at the time. But now, looking back, wow a baby in adult pants. "But yes, oh God. Don't leave substantial real estate and other important things to an inexperienced young adult. It's too much. It's like so much power one day, helplessness the next."

"So telling them you're engaged...gets you off a petition?"

Rose had to laugh. "Getting *married* gets me out of this particular petition. Engaged, no. But it sends a warning flare that my mother understands. Because 'I'm not interested' and 'Leave me alone' doesn't help."

"You really want to stay here that much?"

That was the thing—Rose couldn't say that. Maybe she could live somewhere else if she chose to. If not this city, then a different one, and not where her parents and sisters were. But not being able to say she desperately wanted to stay, left fertile ground for her mother and family to plant their assumptions.

Like: Of course Rose was keen to leave. Of course they should help her settle things in Manila. Even if she never said anything, she of course couldn't want it any other way, could she?

Not having a husband and kids didn't mean her life amounted to nothing. She wasn't sure how to explain it anymore, so she just avoided calls and put off the paperwork.

Now there was a full-on fake fiancé, but her hand had been forced.

Well, not literally. Rose now willingly touched Pascal's hand, put her smaller one in his. She noticed her mom and a tita looking out at them, and she raised their entwined hands and pressed a kiss on his knuckle.

"I want them to leave me alone this much," she muttered into his skin, laughing. But his hand felt good against her lips, and the way he smiled at her, like he couldn't believe she just did that, made her want to do more. "I'm not over-doing it, am I?"

"Rose."

"Sorry. Too much?"

"Oh, no. If you want to kiss other parts of me so it's more convincing, feel free."

"How horny are you? It's been a while, huh?"

Pascal laughed. "A while, but I'm working on my impulse control."

"So this doesn't bother you?"

"Rose, you can kiss me wherever you want."

Well. She didn't quite know what to say to that.

He lifted their hands, the "engagement ring" bright and shiny. "That's a nice ring I got you, by the way."

"It is, isn't it? I felt it just suited me." It was a thin gold band, carrying a single circular diamond. It beamed whenever the porch light hit it at an angle. "I buy myself jewelry. It's such a tita thing to do."

"Convenient for when you need to fake an engagement."

"I'm so smart and prepared that way." Rose had bought two special pieces, to add to the five that she had that were actual gold and diamonds. All the women in her family bought their own jewelry; it was what they did instead of buy cars or houses.

When Rose saw this particular ring, she knew exactly what she would use it for, if she had to, and it was this moment. When she saw it, she thought to herself, this looked like an engagement ring that someone who really knew her would get. It fit her style, her personality, and best of all, she loved looking at it. It felt like it belonged on her finger, never mind who chose it.

"It's late and I've pulled you away from your routine long

enough. Thank you, Pascal. I release you from your service. Good night." Rose hesitated only a beat; he did say she could kiss him. So she did, and swept a soft touch on his mouth, waited, and accepted the kiss he gave back. Then she waved at him and went back into the house.

9

"Pascal, where are you going?"

"Hi, Tita. I was—just getting some air."

Rose's mom, Tita Ramona, caught Pascal before he left the porch. At first he cursed inwardly for taking too long to leave, but realized it was no use. Tita Ramona had been waiting, he was sure of it. Waiting for her moment.

She stepped out onto the porch but didn't sit down. There she was, standing by the front door, at an odd angle that allowed her to see him and eye him from head to foot. This was expert level mom scrutiny, or terror prof posturing. "How are your parents?"

Pascal gave her the standard update.

"And your sister, Tana? She's still with the senator?"

"Yes."

"I meant if she's still seeing him. Did they get married?"

"They're still seeing each other, and they're not married. And they also work together."

Tita Ramona smiled, cracking her guarded exterior a bit. "That's complicated."

"I think they like complicated."

"I was so glad when Rose left politics. Seemed like such a toxic environment to work in for someone so young. Tana is still doing that?"

"Yes. She's—she likes it."

Tita Ramona shrugged. "As long as she's happy. And you, you have your own company? Did I hear that right?"

"I'm not a founder but I'm running operations now especially as things start up."

"Ah. And before that, you...?"

"I taught at Anselmo Graduate School's MBA program. And consulted for business education organizations."

"Ah."

He was an accomplished and confident man, damn it, but when Tita Ramona frowned and shrugged again, after an admittedly weak version of his CV...damn it.

"Because Rose never said anything," Tita Ramona told him. "Not a thing about you. In years. I didn't even think you were friends, or that she thought about you at all."

"We...reconnected recently."

Tita Ramona was still on the level of his strictest professor. "Don't get me wrong, Pascal. I like you. You're a nice boy. You definitely seemed to have grown up okay, very well-educated. There should be nothing wrong with you marrying Rose."

The "but..." was hanging in the air and Pascal let it. He smiled and stayed in his lane.

Tita Ramona's eyes narrowed. "There's this party we're going to and I asked her if she wanted a plus one and she said she didn't."

That made all the sense in the world because Rose didn't have a fiancé at all. "Um, I would go to that party with her if she wants me to."

"So that's how it is?"

"How is what?"

"You just let her tell you what to do."

"What we do together, yeah." Now look here. Pascal lifted his shoulders. *He* had some experience in debate, in recitation, in arguing passionately to an entire audience. He shouldn't be made nervous by *Tita Ramona*. "Tita, I don't know what Rose chooses to tell you about our relationship, but we're consenting adults, and if she is withholding anything I'm sorry but she would have her reasons."

"And that's all right with you? What about what you want to do?"

"I want what she wants." Pascal was on a roll, almost forgetting to check for continuity or consistency. But he believed it? It sounded like something he would say, if he were in a relationship with Rose. "It's that simple."

Her eye twitched, and then relaxed. "Does that mean you're going to the despedida with us?"

"Uh, sure." Pascal blinked. "Yes. If Rose wants me to."

"Fine," Tita Ramona said. "I'll tell them to give us another place at the table. Of course you should be there, if you're going to be family. I have no idea *how* my daughter does relationships but family still means something to me. You'll be there if you say you love her."

"Of course." He would have a lot to explain to Rose tomorrow. "I should go now. Good night, Tita. It was good seeing you again."

Pascal pushed himself off the porch railing, and started walking *away* from the house.

"Hey," Tita Ramona said. "Where are you going?"

Shit. Pascal turned around and wondered how he could do this. It was harder to explain why a fiancé was sleeping in the studio outside wasn't it? That didn't make sense at all. But if he went back in through the front door, he could eventually let himself out to the studio through the kitchen. Yeah, he could do that.

"As you said, you're consenting adults," Tita Ramona said. "You don't have to pretend to be chaste around me. When my friends come over we're usually up until early morning. You don't have to sneak back in. Good night, Pascal. You can go up to the bedroom now. I'm not judging."

10

Sometimes Rose would think about sex, while shampooing her hair. In this big house, the bathroom that she had retiled and fitted with a rain shower head was her second favorite place (the balcony was number one), and where she felt okay letting go. She was alone at home most of the time, but she needed her walls up in the other rooms, for whatever reason. The bedroom where she would usually be, when her family members called her, wasn't spared. The bathroom though? Outside world, who are you.

This time as she massaged shampoo onto her scalp, she thought about kissing, and being kissed. She thought about Pascal's mouth, those firm and plump lips of his, she thought of how it would feel if they were on other parts of her. She let water run down her body and thought of what his hands would feel like on her breasts. It was interesting how this activity, as quick and inconsequential as a daydream, was already by itself enjoyable. Maybe Rose loved this part, a close second to actually finding satisfaction in sex. The warm water, the comfortable space, a memory, anticipation. Feeling things could be pleasant. In here, she could control it.

Her closet was in her bedroom, so she wrapped her towel around her body and padded out of her bath.

And found Pascal *right there*, right where her bedroom led out to her balcony.

"I'm sorry," he said, jumping one step closer to her, waving his hands. His volume level was a theatrical whisper. "I'm really sorry. Your mom made me come up here."

"*What?*"

"She watched me go up the stairs! She insisted that we don't need to hide that we're sharing a room."

"Oh shit." Her mom was diabolical. "So you didn't go to the studio at all?"

He laughed. "No, I committed to the cover story and came up here."

"And here you are." Rose tightened the towel wrapped around her and wiped moisture from her forehead. She couldn't be sweating already, right after her bath. And it had been so refreshing. "Pascal, you didn't have to—"

"It's fine. I can hang out on the balcony for a bit, right? You can do your thing, just ignore me."

"Pascal. My mom and her friends will be talking and eating and drinking until dawn. That's what they do. You think you're giving them ten minutes and then you'll go back down and make it outside without being noticed? It's not going to be ten minutes."

"I guess I'm stuck here then."

"No, you're not." Rose sighed. "You don't have to be. You can absolutely head back down to your actual room and never mind if I have to tell my mom that I lied to her. It's been a long night already."

Pascal took two steps backward, bringing him out to the

balcony, and then he looked over his shoulder, toward the railing.

Rose laughed. "It's too high."

"I'm very athletic."

"Don't fucking jump from my balcony just to avoid confessing to my mom! It's not that big a deal." Rose pressed her palm to her forehead. Yeah, this was cute for the duration of dinner but planning this escape was not as fun. "Pascal. Come back in here."

"I'm not going to jump." What he did was walk back into her bedroom, and immediately Rose's body buzzed with awareness. Of her near nudity, of how she was relieved that she wasn't calling an ambulance for him because of some ill-conceived stunt. Pascal said, "If you let me stay here tonight, I can do that. I'll sit on your lounge chair. It looks very comfortable. I can slip out at dawn. Your mom has to sleep sometime."

"But—"

"You can send me to another room up here. There are a few."

Rose shook her head. "Yeah and then they'll run into you coming out of my home office? Might as well give up right now. You can stay in here with me."

"I really don't mind, and I won't bother you. I have stuff to read and watch anyway."

"You're not bothering me. I'm grateful for tonight as it is." Not even an hour ago, she was enjoying kissing and touching this man, and now he was in her bedroom. "You can shower here, and I'll have clothes you can use. And you can read or watch whatever on the bed."

"With you?"

"It's large. It's comfortable." Amazing how casual she

sounded, like she offered one side of her bed to men all the time. Just to hang out. "And you're *not* sitting on my balcony chair. That's mine."

11

"I'm getting sleepy."

"Oh, go ahead. You can sleep."

Well of course Rose didn't need permission to fall asleep on her own bed, but Pascal thought it was good to mention it. She might have been worried about falling asleep right next to someone she knew briefly twenty years ago, and then was suddenly living downstairs. It made sense for her to not completely let her guard down. But how about *his* guard though? His was almost all the way down. Practically no guard.

Not advisable.

He'd even let her be part of the very thing that made him relax and unwind the most, and he *never* shared this with anyone. For the past hour or so that they'd been watching his favorite soothing YouTube channel of expert chefs making sushi, using his phone, she was actually snuggling a bit against him, and he welcomed it. Welcomed it like every little thing she'd offered since he came up into her room. From the use of her bathroom that gave him the best shower he'd had in years (like he was a kid under a warm, controlled fall of rain), to the stack of neatly folded and new clothes he could wear after, the bottle of water waiting on a table beside "his" side of the bed, sharing the Wi-Fi password.

He was shocked at the hospitality but she brushed it off, saying she was used to it, from renting out the studio the past few years. Pascal doubted that the privileges of renting extended to her most awesome bathroom, but she obviously didn't want to make a big deal out of it.

He understood the language of I Don't Need Help and This Is Not Help.

At some point during their sushi binge-watch, she tucked her head into his neck, their legs side by side. A few times he checked if she was still awake and she was, but sleep or fatigue was definitely settling in.

"You can sleep on my shoulder," Pascal said. "You...you feel good."

"No, *you* feel good. Like a cozy pillow."

He laughed softly.

"Cozy, dense, muscley pillow." Her arm stretched across his torso, then she actually squeezed him like he was a pillow. "I'm *really* sorry about tonight, Pascal. I haven't figured out their schedule while they're here but it's always packed. You probably won't see them again while they're in town anyway. And when you're at work then you're at work. I mean I don't see you at all during the week anyway."

"That's a choice." Pascal would be dropping by the house more just to see her, if she would let him. It didn't have to be about what he could get from the kitchen or any other room in the house. Hanging out with her was fun. "I thought we'd established...lines. And the studio's really comfortable, I really have been just staying in there."

"Right, I drew lines, didn't I? And then erased them. I'm

really sorry. You can go back to your regular life tomorrow. I won't bother you about this again."

"You keep apologizing. It's not a problem at all."

Her fingers played with the material of the shirt he was wearing, the shirt she gave him. A soft and comfortable fabric, but as her fingertips scraped and drummed, his body reacted like she was doing that directly on his skin. "You probably get tita comments about your relationship status a lot."

"All that and they also tell me I need to grow up."

"You're a fully grown man!"

"Yeah but they think I was in school way too long. They want me to get a real job, own things, have kids."

"And that's the strangest thing, isn't it? We're at that age, when *they* were telling Younger Us to do all that. We're tito and tita age. If we've made different choices, there's a reason for it."

"Oh they just think we missed the memo. We should be reminded often and strongly."

"It won't end, you know. I might have shut up one line of questioning when we lied about being engaged but it just opens the next line. When's the wedding? When will you have kids? Now is better, then have another." Rose groaned and pressed her face against his chest. "Make it stop."

"I know what you mean." It was one of those rare times when a shared annoyance made him feel more bonded to someone than actual blood. "Fuck them."

Rose's laugh was now practically his, the way she softly vibrated right on him. She moved her head, and they were face to face. Close enough to see the pink of her parted lips, right before they pressed against his. She was purring into this sleepy, sloppy, delicious kiss, but then it didn't remain sleepy or sloppy for long. Pascal felt his pulse, felt his awareness wake up. And hers as well. The next kiss was full, and knowing. He touched her face, touched her hair, found where on her head to cradle her as he kissed her and slid her down into her pillow, down on the bed. Rose sighed, or gasped, or giggled—it sounded like all of it.

"Oh my *God*." Rose disengaged, sat up, and looked at him like she'd been suddenly jolted from sleep.

He was not sure if that was a good thing, but one of her hands was still on his chest, the other touching her lips. "Rose, we don't have to."

She nodded a little vigorously. "We won't, not right now anyway. But that's not it. I just had this weird feeling that I was disappointing my mother, making out with a guy in secret in her house. I'm forty-one years old!"

"Yes you are."

"And it's *my* house!" Rose glared rebelliously at no one in particular. "Who cares if they can hear me right now?"

"They all know I went up here. They're probably expecting sounds."

"Exactly!" And then she let go, and started laughing for real. It was a laugh that dug deep, and he could practically see the stress roll off her. Pascal was hit not just with desire on top of current arousal, but envy too. When did he last laugh like that? When did he last feel that good and absolutely done with shit? Maybe that would have helped center himself better in the last few years, because he was just angry a lot. And tired a lot. Letting go felt like prying resentment out of his hands when he wasn't ready to.

When their eyes met again, hers was bright with laughter. "Well, not the sounds. The room's large enough and they'd need to have their ear at the door and we'd have to be *super loud*...anyway I'm sure they think we're having lots of sex."

"...and they would be wrong. I know you're exhausted. Go right ahead and sleep. I'll make my way to the studio as soon as the titas leave."

12

Pascal heard the cars belonging to the titas leave sometime before dawn, but didn't get up until the sun had come up. Rose was sleeping soundly near the middle of the bed, curled up and facing him in a way that seemed like trust but also self-protection. Pascal didn't get a lot of space to himself, but he had been comfortable.

There was something familiar about waking up in the room, but it made sense because the sheets smelled the same as the ones in the studio. And they were facing the same direction, so they experienced the sun the same way. Only been a few weeks since he started living here but there were all these little reminders of how he might have been living like a slob before. Not a huge slob, but...his conditions could be better.

For example, he didn't care about blankets but Rose's studio provided a thick woolly one apart from the flat sheet over the bed and it was *soft*. Like a goddamn hug.

He thought of kissing her before he left, but the way her face was squished into her pillow wasn't convenient. Even thinking of that made him laugh a little to himself; he always left at the appointed time, without saying goodbye. He established that early, when he started dating, seeing people, having sex. *Set the agenda and don't deviate.* Pascal knew to follow his own advice. Setting expectations early had always worked for him.

He did not expect the two very awake people in the kitchen.

"Oh my God, it's really you!"

Rose's two sisters were on stools at the center island, making sandwiches. One of them had short and curly hair that was a gold-brown shade, one was taller and her dark hair was full and straight and showed the beginnings of gray. They'd be late twenties to mid thirties by now, and Pascal was slightly irritated at himself for not even checking with Rose about this. He did recognize them, though. Like, he knew that the one who had talked to him, with the shorter hair, was the youngest.

"Carly," she said, bright and sunny as a Manila morning. "Do you remember me? I was a fetus when you were coming over here."

"She was probably ten or eleven," the more somber sister, Annika apparently, corrected. "And it's Pascal, right? Pascal Cortes. Ate Tana's younger brother."

"That...that's right. All of it." Damn. Pascal was so close to the door, to the studio, and now this.

"He's wearing Ate Rose's clothes," Carly pointed a bread knife at him. "That's sweet. You wear Zora/Maya all the time? That's so supportive of you."

Pascal realized he had left his actual clothes from before he showered up at Rose's room, and maybe it was for the best. "Yeah, it's their clothes. These are really comfortable. And, uh, I didn't expect both of you to be up so early."

Carly shrugged. "Jet lag. Do you want a sandwich? I've

already had three. Oh my God, do you know how much I've missed this peanut butter? Look at that oil, yum." From out of the small jar she pulled her knife, a clump of chunky peanut butter clinging to it, oil dripping down the blade, the handle, and right onto the counter.

"*Carly*," her older sister said.

Pascal blinked. "Oh, I don't need a sandwich—"

"Are you sneaking out?" Annika's eyes narrowed. "Do you not live here?"

"I don't *live* here. I have my own place."

"Obviously, he stays over for, you know, sex stuff. That's great. I was a little concerned for Ate Rose but I'm glad she's getting some. I mean, some, or a lot, no judgment. All up to you." Carly was completely amused by her own words. "I wonder what Mom will say. Did she talk to you? I'm sure she'd end up talking to you. She liked you back then, Pascal."

"We talked for a few minutes last night. I guess this is all sudden."

"Mom's plans for Ate Rose are totally screwed." Carly was laughing as she continued making her sandwich. "Oh my God, I'm gonna laugh now because I won't be able to when Mom is actually around. Holy shit."

Annika shook her head. "Ate Rose gets to make her own plans. Pascal being here doesn't change that."

"She just said they're engaged, Ate Annika."

"They're not married."

Carly giggled as she spread more peanut butter on her bread. "Who cares if they get married? Shots fired, Ate Rose is not on board with Mom's plan. Y'all are hilarious."

Pascal had enough of a briefing from Rose to know that there was immigration-related family drama, and it was best for him to play his part and not say anything to ruin things.

He also hadn't read up on the law that covered Rose's case as much as every single family member here seemed to, and it was going to be obvious if he tried to fake it. Also, he was sleepy, and was thinking of what was the best excuse to go to the studio and stay inside it for several hours. He could say he had stuff in there, right? And he needed to go to his sister's place anyway.

"I have to go," Pascal said. "I have to be at Tana's for breakfast. But enjoy your peanut butter."

"Yeah I'm taking off too!" Carly said. "Suddenly super sleepy. Night all. Night, new brother."

Annika didn't move from her spot and just watched her sister leave. Then she leaned toward Pascal, before he could leave too. "You need to think about how you really want to play this out, Pascal."

"Excuse me?"

"You can't really be engaged to Rose."

"I am. There's a ring."

"Whatever. She can buy her own ring. I talk to her several times a week for years. On weekends she's taking my call alone on her balcony. She's never said a thing about you, and if you've just been hiding all this time, you're strangely absent on date nights and special occasions. When did you even show up again? Aren't you like in school or something?"

"I was. Because I was teaching. Is it hard to believe I'd be completely in love with your sister and want to be with her forever?"

"That's not it at all," Annika scoffed. "Rose is awesome and *you'd* want to love her and be with her, sure. She just never acted like *this*—" and she waved at him "—was what she wanted. She already has a place to live. And a career she seems to enjoy. I'm sure if she had *needs* she has her ways."

"It's early so I'll let all of that not offend me in any way," Pascal said. "Also, you're right to be concerned. You're not the first person to think I don't have much to offer in terms of long-term relationships."

Annika might have shuddered, if he interpreted the subtle shake of her shoulders that way. "Well, like Carly said, I don't care what it is you give her as long as it's what she wants you to. And we can change the topic now even if it's sudden. I'm just saying, I don't believe for a second that you're actually engaged, but I'm gonna go with it because I do think Ate Rose deserves to be left alone if that's what she wants. And can you tell her that? Tell her I'm on her side."

"Why can't *you* tell her that yourself?"

"Do you think clear and honest communication between her and our mother has led to this moment? You probably don't know a lot of what's been going on, and I'm not going to be the one to tell you. But just...let her know that it doesn't have to be like this, okay?"

Pascal cleared his throat. "Sure, I will tell my fiancée that." Annika could say what she wanted, but Pascal was not going to drop the act until Rose let him. "If it comes up."

"Your fiancée."

"Yeah."

"Great. Will I see you again here anytime this week?"

"I'm back here tonight," Pascal admitted. "Or earlier." Because he actually did live here, at least for three more weeks.

"Will you be at the despedida we're attending?"

"Yes."

"Will you be at the surprise party we're having for Mom's birthday?"

"I don't—" He did not know that was a thing, but it made sense that he'd be there. "Of course."

“It’s why we’re here too. Mom was getting antsy, was saying she wants to spend her 65th with her friends.”

“Then of course I’ll be there.”

Annika’s glare was a lot for this time of day. “As Rose’s fiancé.”

“Which is what I am.”

She huffed. “You say that now.”

13

"Those three?" Pascal's eleven-year-old niece Viv mouthed the words, because she knew she wasn't supposed to let the opposing players find out what his Pusoy Dos strategy was.

Pascal shook his head, frowned a little. Viv wanted to know if he was going to play his trio of sevens, but he wouldn't, not this turn. He had better chances putting it into a full house.

But then his sister Tana put down a full house with a trio of nines, which nixed his plan. And then David, Tana's boyfriend, followed that with a full jack.

Viv peeked at his hand and stifled a laugh.

"Is Tito Pascal gonna lose?" His sister teased.

Pascal *did* lose, and endured a minute of his niece explaining to him why it happened. He held on to the sevens for too long, without a pair. And then eventually, he needed to break it up and played a pair, and was left with a middling card that he couldn't play on its own or with anything else. He knew this but let the girl rub it in.

"You think she should be learning this at her age?"

Pascal asked the other adults at the table.

Tana laughed. "We learned it when we were younger than her."

Shit, they did. Pascal was feeling this way too often now. Having lived a lot, and not enough. "You should maybe update the parenting standards, I don't know."

That was a joke, of course. Tana was an exceptional parent, though even she would admit that she wasn't sure about it in the beginning. Pascal saw all eleven years of it and the pregnancy, and it did seem difficult but also...somewhat cool. Not that he was looking for the same responsibility himself but Viv was a delight to be around, and she seemed to like him too.

"Are you wearing Rose's shirt?" Tana was saying, as she cleared the table of cards.

"Yeah, I've worn two of the shirts so far. It's great."

"It *is*, isn't it? I wear the tops to work all the time. David and his staff had a custom set made. They wear Zora/Maya on Tuesdays and Thursdays."

Pascal had actually noticed that. He wasn't surprised that David and Tana would be supporting a business like Rose's. Apart from being friends, that was totally their thing. His sister could be ruthless in the way that people who worked in politics had to be, but also drew lots of lines and ethical boundaries. She'd be on the side of local industry and fashion.

"You look good, Tito Pascal," Viv was nice enough to say. "Fresh."

"What does that mean? I wasn't before?"

Tana snickered. "Maybe it's because we're finally seeing you in something else."

"I think you can explain exactly what you mean yourself, Viv."

The girl smiled widely. "We don't see you in anything new."

"I buy new clothes."

"That look exactly like your old clothes."

"I can't have my own style?"

"You can! It's just boring."

"I'm sure you share the same opinion," Pascal directed to his sister.

Tana shrugged. "Yes, but I didn't bother to say anything because I don't actually care that much about it. It's cute that she mentioned it to you."

"They asked me to model for their website. Maybe I'll get free clothes."

"Pascal." Her eyebrow quirked. "Come help me get the sandwiches."

"I'll help," Viv offered.

"No." Tana winked at her daughter. "I'm about to have a sibling-only conversation with my brother."

Why did she even bother to take him aside when she would tell David and Viv about this anyway? Pascal had that impression every time he stepped into this household. They were a single unit composed of three persons. And only David, ironically the only person here who was a national legislator, bossed him around the least.

"Pascal."

His sister and her family did not live in a big house as expected of a senator's family. It was instead a three-bedroom townhouse that was less than an hour's drive from where they worked. It was comfortable, but nothing like the Alban house where the kitchen was practically its own universe. This space was not huge. "Yes, Ate?"

"What's going on there?"

"Where?"

"At Rose's."

"You mean where I'm staying. I'm opening the Pisara office. Working. You know what I'm doing there."

"And you and Rose are getting along?"

The tone wasn't angry or scolding. This was Tana fishing for chismis. "We're cool."

"Yeah?"

"What did you think I was going to say?"

Tana approached the counter with a little can of parmesan cheese, shaking it over meatball sandwiches and little pizzas. "I'm just taking note of the modeling, the outfits, and how you both seem to still be on speaking terms after how many weeks?"

"Two-ish. And of course we're still on speaking terms. I barely see her when it's the work week."

Tana's laugh bubbled. "Maybe that's the key to a lasting harmonious relationship with you, Pascal."

She was taunting him. Well, this lack of faith—even jokingly—was going to cost her. Maybe he wouldn't tell her that he was already fake engaged to her friend. If she hadn't been such a joker, they could be having a more interesting conversation right now. She'd find out sooner that he was being an excellent accomplice to Rose and sending him to her studio rental was the best idea Tana ever had. Or a close second if one considered the daily brilliance required of her from working for the senator.

But—maybe it was better that they weren't talking about this. Maybe Rose wouldn't want the fake engagement news to go out beyond the people she'd originally intended to deceive. Maybe he shouldn't go around bragging about a situation he only fell into because he was conveniently around.

"Yeah, that's it exactly," he said.

14

By now, Rose didn't need to tell the story all over again, but in her twenties, it was all anyone who knew her wanted to ask about. Oh, her family had immigrated? But without her? When was she supposed to "follow"? What was it like, being "abandoned"?

The choice of words had always been jarring, sometimes offensive, and Rose had learned several hundred instances ago to not say anything. Admitting her real feelings never landed right, because those asking were projecting. *They* would feel abandoned, if it were them. *They* would be fixated on following *by any means necessary*, if they had been in her position. To admit that she actually didn't mind the sudden independence made her seem ungrateful.

It was easier to shut up, and even when technology put into her hands the ability to see and call her parents at any time, the distance and time zones and being busy with life made it easy to avoid having this conversation.

It felt like she had been having it for literal decades.

"That young man wanted to meet you," Rose's mom was saying. "He'd actually heard of your business. Saw an article about you and Ana Cuadrado online. He really wanted to meet you."

Rose took a deep fortifying breath and imagined the dining table not as it currently was, but how it tended to be when she was working. Even when the table was cluttered it was thoughtfully so, and she liked looking at it. And her favorite sound was hearing sharp shears cut straight through cloth. That satisfying rip, then flutter of color.

She went to that place in her mind for a few moments as she watched her mom say those things again. Like it was her fault that this setup she didn't ask for—Rose didn't even know *which guy* her mom was talking about—was not going to happen. The visualization exercise was relaxing, sure, but her mom's rant wasn't causing Rose any anxiety or distress right now.

Rose was imagining fluttering cloth because she was horny.

"I'm sorry." When Rose spoke she was calm. Her mom was jet-lagged, spent all night partying, and it had been over a year since they were actually in the same country, the same house. This should be a happier time. Mrs. Alban shouldn't spend this visit talking about some guy Rose didn't want to meet.

But whose fault was that? Her mom kept the trip a secret and showed up unannounced.

"You're *not* sorry," Mrs. Alban said, pressing the sponge that had her powder onto her nose three times. "Of course you're not sorry, bringing out Pascal like that."

"You surprised me. And he was here."

"You couldn't have said this the many times I asked?"

Rose cleared her throat. "Said what?"

"That you're engaged!"

"What would it change?"

"Everything! You're not really engaged, are you?"

"I said I am. You saw me and Pascal."

Her mom's shoulders shook. "Yes that was quite a performance. Don't be surprised that I'm suspicious when you didn't say *a thing* about this. He's a good guy. You didn't have to hide it."

"I don't know. It just felt like something I didn't want to announce first, you know? Because there are just too many *plans*." She folded her arms.

"The plan is *for you*. Your future."

The *plan* was nebulous and abstract but Rose understood its concept. It was a general plan to get Rose to the US by whatever means necessary. Sometimes it was in the form of a news article, about new jobs she might qualify for somewhere. Other times, it was a friend with a business promising some sketchy type of employment. Another form of the plan looked a lot like matchmaking, more frequently since she turned thirty-five. Rose was keenly aware that her mother was chatting up friends, looking for their bachelor sons and grandsons, anyone over twenty-five and with a job was a possibility. At first Rose said "no" loudly and clearly...later on, she got tired of even responding.

Sometimes, a tiny voice inside wondered if she would ever change her mind, give up the resistance one day. Would she cave, and let their good intentions take over? Would she actually say yes to one call, one date, with someone whose main draw was his citizenship?

And then again, in a flash that struck through her entire body for the nth time today, a memory of Pascal's mouth on hers, that huge body of his hot and cozy against her back, and...

Rose cleared her throat. "Thank you, Mom, as always. For thinking of me. But I'm with Pascal now."

"What's his status? Do you know?"

"Engaged to me?"

Mrs. Alban frowned, this time applying lipstick with exaggerated frustration. "I mean what's his citizenship?"

"Filipino."

"Not dual anything? Didn't his sister study abroad before?"

"Tana was in the US and UK on student visas, but Pascal stayed here." Actually, she didn't *know* what passports he carried but she had a narrative and she was sticking to it. "He's always been here."

"You can put your wedding plans on hold, and then petition him as fiancé."

Of course her mom would say that. Given enough time to reflect on this Ramona Alban would be able to redo *the plan* entirely—as she had already done many times. It was probably her favorite hobby.

"Mom—"

"He'll do it if he loves you. What kind of delay would that be? Just a few more years."

That was in its own way reasonable, what her mom was suggesting, *if* Rose were still, say, twenty-five. At forty-one, "if he loves you, he'll wait for his visa to get approved," was an actual sentence that didn't have the effect that it used to. What was the point?

Also, they weren't actually engaged.

This argument was built on broken foundations.

"If we do that you shouldn't suddenly elope, you understand?" Not surprisingly Mrs. Alban was totally into this new plan that she had pivoted to, and Rose's input wasn't required anymore. "Live together if you want. You probably already are, anyway. But no legal paperwork. You have to remain unmarried upon approval and then I can look up the requirements for the fiancé visa—"

Maybe Rose should shut up a little while longer this time, she thought. This hobby kept her mom's mind sharp, even if it was at the expense of Rose's future, and freedom to choose it for herself, and well...what was the harm in letting her look up a list of documents? At least it was an exercise in internet literacy.

Rose and Pascal could "break up" at some determined future time and it would be sad but understandable (they'd think Rose did something to scare him off), and things would go back to square one. At least her mom would have had some days of distraction.

Rose's hands warmed. Could hands do that? Could they blush? Because this time she was remembering touching Pascal's chest, wanting badly to do it again. It was all this talk of him being her fiancé. It set off a thought pattern of things couples did. Dates. Dinner. Meeting the family. Pascal pushing her up against a wall and pounding—

"Definitely not the F3 or F4," her mom was saying.

Rose blinked and cleared her throat. "Uh, why not?"

"It's a twenty-year wait. Or more. Which would have been fine if you had gotten married twenty years ago...or we could write a letter so your status could maybe be updated and the years in process just carry over..."

Rose laughed. "Mom."

"I would rather *not* have you be filed as F4, is what I'm saying. It'll take too long."

"It's already been very long." Almost two decades since they'd been living in separate countries. An entire young adult's life. Three presidential terms. Entire epic TV series premiered and ended. The world had already changed several times over. Time could be quick or syrupy slow, depending on where she wanted to stay, which view she was looking at. "And Pascal is here."

Pascal is here, holy shit. That wasn't just her reiterating the fake engagement story—Pascal was actually physically there, unlocking the gate in his way, that she could now tell by the way it sounded, by how he let the latch fall. She knew he planned to leave her room by sunrise and that she wouldn't see him when she woke up. Rose knew that, and expected it, and still huffed with disappointment and walked around all day wanting release.

"Anyway, he's here." Rose said. "What time will you be back tonight?"

Her mom looked out, in the direction of her future son-in-law, with some suspicion still. "Late. Your Tita Susan will take me to a concert and then cake after."

"Of course. Enjoy."

The sound Rose heard in response was a lot like *hmph*, but she found an excuse to ignore it. She had a fiancé to greet, and she had to intercept him before he went into the studio first, and give her mom even more reason to suspect shenanigans. Without saying where she was going, she went out into the driveway, and let nature take its course.

Meaning, she pretty much flung herself at him. Skipped and hopped right into those arms, before she could figure out what to say to warn him.

"Babe." Maybe he didn't need warning? Pascal shifted a bag he had been carrying to swing toward his back and scooped her right up. Dropped a kiss on her forehead and pressed their faces together nose to nose.

"She's watching us?" She asked him, so she wouldn't have to turn around to do it. But Rose *knew* her mom was looking.

Pascal laughed and spoke into her cheek. "Absolutely."

"We should kiss."

"If we must." Pascal started it, bending to put himself in the best position to give her an indulgent open-mouthed kiss, the kind that left her breathless and longing and all kinds of hot. Rose appreciated that he went first because the *optics* were better that way, and for a second it might look to her mom that this was a hot guy who actually was engaged to her. Imagine that.

Anyway—this was a good kiss, yay optics, and still a kiss that Rose wanted. Yes please, her mouth and hands and body seemed to say, more of that, right over there, please consume me completely. The annoying hovering mood of dissatisfaction that had bothered her all day was all but gone, conspicuously paused. Anticipating satisfaction.

Wait...she could just have it. They could just do it. The only person she needed to consult on the matter was already present. She could just pull her mouth away from his to ask him.

How simple. Convenient.

They'd need to get out of the front yard though, but maybe Pascal was a step ahead thinking of that too, because Rose was now kissing him while walking backwards, being steered by him to what she knew to be the studio. He managed to do this *and* unlock the door *and* slam it shut and Rose stopped moving only when the wall met her back. And there it was, the delicious feeling of being completely surrounded by him. Rose's desire was awake and hungry; the slightest friction from her needy tentative grind against his erection was the best thing she'd felt today. Top sensation. 10/10.

"You want more, Rose?"

Yes, more. That was the intention. It might have started as a kiss to keep up appearances but that was an excuse at best. The reason was right here, the thing she was about to say.

"Yeah. Pascal, I kind of want to fuck."

He paused, and then laughed, again. "Kind of?"

Rose was being cute when she said that—she didn't mean "kind of" at all. "Not just 'kind of', sorry. I mean definitely. For sure. Right now, if you have time."

"Yes." He was still laughing softly. "I have time. Your mom isn't going to knock all of a sudden?"

"She's leaving for a thing with her friends. She should have left by now. You have condoms anywhere here?"

Pascal reached for something in his back pocket. A box, new. "I may have wanted the same."

"Love it when priorities align. Now, please." This was probably not the most graceful thing she ever did, but Rose got rid of her panties and shorts and it seemed like she did it really quickly. "Yes, when I say now I mean now, against this wall. You okay with it?"

"Since you asked."

Rose rolled her head back to rest against the wall, maybe to find some stability, maybe to stop herself from getting too overwhelmed over realizing that a fantasy of hers might be happening for real right now. A quick fuck against the wall. Maybe she wasn't lucky but it had been difficult to get anyone to do this with. Also sometimes the logistics and location just didn't work out. But here they were. Pascal released his cock from his jeans and boxers, and for a moment the bare skin of its head slid against her skin. Smooth and hot. And then covered up by a condom, and then in his hand, being guided into her. Her pussy was wet, had been all day, it felt like. Did he need to go that slow? Rose let out a sound that reminded her of a frustrated animal—oh God she would have been embarrassed if she weren't so *frustrated*—and when he pushed into her she dug her fingers into his shoulders and took him all the way in.

It felt great.

"*Yes.*" She couldn't have been more thankful. And wow, was he handsome. Even when he looked pained and ready to come but they'd only just started so he was trying to pull himself together. His hand touched her face, before he braced it against the wall. Then he pumped once, long and slow.

"*No,*" Rose groaned. "Faster."

"I was thinking about you all day," he muttered, not moving, deep inside her. "I was thinking about how you smell, how your body felt when I woke up. I'm so hard. I'll come so soon."

"Marathon sex is a nice concept for next time. Now please let's just fuck."

"I don't want to come before you do."

"Just *trust* me and go hard and fast and now."

His next stroke was hard but not hard enough, fast but not fast enough, and Rose told him just how much harder, how much faster, and it didn't take long. She let go, and came as he pounded them against the wall, and he came with a strangled whimper soon after she did.

It was exactly as she wanted it.

15

"Should we talk about this?" he heard her say.

"Yeah, sure." He had just gone into the bathroom to throw the condom and clean up, and by the time he stepped back out, she was drying her hands on a paper towel, doing a thing to her hair in front of the mirror. Her clothes were all back to presentable, but her cheeks and neck were still flushed.

"I feel like I sounded really desperate and needy, haha." Rose was smiling and also cringing a little. "I...have no excuse? I was horny."

"Please. I showed up with condoms in my jeans pocket. And I've been horny all day."

"Okay, so...we're good?" She blinked at him. "You don't, um, regret this?"

"Absolutely not. You're hot." And she absolutely was. Pascal was reminded of that first night hanging out at the balcony, that moment when he saw Rose lean back and stretch. There was something about her looking relaxed, like she was floating. Gorgeous.

"Thank you. You are too. You're, like, a hotter hookup than I thought I'd have access to, you know. At this time."

"What are you talking about...?"

"You want coffee while we talk about this? We can go to the house."

"You sure about that? We can keep talking in here, if someone might overhear—"

She waved a hand. "It's *my* house. I can bring you up if I want to. And they're all out by now, so we'll have it to ourselves."

A statement of fact, that was all, and the way it made him think of more sex right after having it was all on him. But merienda at the house was not a consolation prize because in minutes, they were having cold melon juice and pulling various pastries out of boxes that lined the dining table. At least half a dozen boxes in all, and when he lifted one lid, there was something else inside. Little croissants. Flavored pandesal. Brownies. They surrounded a basket of assorted fresh fruit—bananas, watermelons, papayas, pineapples, occupying the center of the table.

"Is it like this here every weekend?" Pascal had been heading back to his own place on the weekends so far, or just staying in the studio. Did not realize he was missing a feast. "Who eats all of this?"

"I subscribed to a service that delivers the fruit basket every Saturday. Local farmers and whatever's in season. The pastries are probably my mom and sisters picking stuff up wherever they went."

"Even the fruit basket is a *lot*."

Rose raised her glass. "Why I make a lot of juice."

They picked their merienda and set up at the center island in the kitchen. Clearer space and a lot cozier. Also with a full view of the driveway and they could quickly change their topic of conversation if someone else were to show up. He was pretty sure this was "the talk" that no one else newly inhabiting the house should be overhearing.

"So, the sex thing," Rose continued, as breezy as if she had asked if he wanted more juice. "It was hot and satisfying, right? Like, honestly?"

"Yes—absolutely. Honestly."

"Okay, awesome," she said, her face still glowing and now also looking relieved. "I mean you know this, you heard it from everyone I guess. I'm still getting used to the idea that we can have it great right now. Even at 'our age.'"

"Because they think we're getting old?"

"Because we're told to dread turning forty. Like we've missed something if we're not married or with a kid or—or if we're living here. In this country." She shrugged. "Is that just me?"

"Definitely not just you."

"I can't help but think we were all getting played because the past few years that I've ignored all their plans I've been feeling *great*. Things are scary, and there are so many problems we *collectively* need to fix, but I believe in my decisions now, you know? It took a long time but now I do, and it was really important to me to get to this point. I'm not waiting to be 'saved.'"

For years, Pascal was always too young to be considered for the career he wanted, and he did rely on being "saved"—for someone to notice he'd been doing the work and eventually reward him for it. Then seemingly overnight, he was the right age but didn't *have* the experience, because he never got the jobs.

Someone like him already had a lot of privilege in business school as it was, so he couldn't complain, but the path he had been on was deliberately narrowed and he knew he had to go do something else. "I know what you mean. Decisions feel real now."

"Decisions feel *solid*. I can see the effect on actual lives, not just mine. I like seeing the positive impact of things. And I'm less patient when something feels like a scam. For example, career. I spent so much time trying to find a political comms job that I didn't hate, and I realized maybe I hate all of it. Maybe nothing would ever feel good to me about that life again."

"So now you started the fashion business."

"So now I'm *overseeing* a business that sustains a community but with fashion as its main product. I'm not a fashion or retail expert just yet."

"I'm not a school administrator, but it feels like I'm about to be."

"Do you like what you're doing?"

"Yes." Pascal answered that quickly, but it was also true.

"Funny. And we couldn't have done this earlier, could we? Some people know what they want the first time. We had to spend years doing something else."

"Yeah, what do they think they are? In a race or something?"

They both laughed, and he liked that. "Pascal," she said. "You're okay."

He liked hearing that too. "Thanks."

"You really are. You are definitely way better than what they said I'd have to settle for if I'm still single at this age. Did my mom or sister say anything about that? When they got you alone? I have a feeling they'd say something about that."

"A little. But you don't need people telling you that you need to settle."

"No, they tell me I *will* settle. Like it's gravity or getting wet when it rains. So the idea of you being around for a little while...I think it's cute."

Pascal wouldn't have said cute but this was the most fun he'd had in a while. "It's fun."

"I'm glad you said that. And you'll stick around, right? You'll stick around as my fiancé while they're here?"

"Not a problem."

"Awesome. That's great. I just don't believe it's sustainable in the long run."

"What?" Pascal thought he'd misheard her, but she kept right on, obviously saying exactly what he'd heard.

"...I don't think either of us has actual time to give to a real relationship, and I'm shocked I didn't just front a fake fiancé before now. This is really so much more efficient and does the job without the actual *relationship* work, you know? I have so much going on. And *you* have so much going on. In the past two weeks you were already living here, but we barely saw each other and it was okay."

"That was because I was avoiding—because boundaries—"

"I'm not saying that's bad. They make it sound like I'm sad here in this house alone, but I'm not complaining. Getting to own this and live here is a responsibility, and a privilege. If I long for company it's because I have very specific desires sometimes, but I never complain about having this house."

Pascal flashed back to past conversations, all his friends saying they didn't need or want relationships. Time and circumstance led some to change their minds eventually, but Rose right now? Sounded like she really did mean it. The woman had everything she needed. He, or someone like him, was not part of that list at all.

Which was fine, right? This was what he said he wanted?

No pressure, no strings, someone who would let him put his work first.

This was...

"I understand," Pascal said. "This is only what we need it to be and nothing more."

"Yeah," Rose said. "This is what you were looking for, right? Because you don't have time for—" her hands gestured, forming a big circle "—something major. Something disruptive. Just keep doing what we like. So I have some suggestions."

"Suggestions."

"Move into my room while my mom's here. And you can move your stuff too, so you're not sneaking into the studio to get them. If you need privacy, or just time away from me, stay in the studio anytime."

"Are you sure? It's your room. And my work schedule isn't regular yet. Sometimes I leave really early, sometimes I'm here in the middle of the day."

Rose nodded, getting more into it. "See, I actually think that's better? I set my own work hours too, and don't really have time to monitor whether you're here or not. But if you're home and going up to my room I at least don't have to plan 'couple time' with you that they can see. Even when we're not together it'll count as couple time."

"You know they suspect we're not actually together."

"This is beyond the technicality of whether you're really marrying me or not. I want them to see you walking into my bedroom like you belong there. It might make them stop finding guys I could marry or ridiculous jobs I should take for a green card, for like a year."

Pascal had to laugh a little. "I'm happy to help. But it's your room, your space. I don't want to intrude."

"It's my house. I have a comfy home office to occupy if I

need time away from you. The closest bathroom is the one in my bedroom so you'll have to use it but same drill as my rules for the studio bathroom—keep it clean. Identical box of supplies under the sink. And you're not the only guy who's ever slept on a bed with me. What you *don't* sit on is my balcony chair, that's mine. You're not intruding. It's cool, I promise."

"Well," he said. "Now that you promised. That's binding."

"Please. You on my bed is less stressful for me than constantly watching out for where my mom is and what she's planning. But that's if you don't mind. I understand if this is too weird for you and that's all you need to say."

"I...I don't mind." Her room was large and comfortable and the bathroom was heaven. "I'll still pay you rent."

"Of course. And we have sex whenever we want."

He nodded. "I wholeheartedly agree."

"Do you know what your plans are at the end of our lease agreement?"

Plans? Pisara EdTech would be fully open by then, and Pascal had proposed the five week lease of her studio assuming he'd be able to ease into a regular schedule and go back to his own place after that.

"I was just going to move back to my apartment," he said.

Rose paused as she sipped her juice. She licked her lips after, slowly. "That's a good thing, I think."

"A good thing because you'll want the dude out of your house as soon as possible?"

"A good thing because you promised yourself you wouldn't Fuck It Up or whatever this year and this shouldn't change that. You have a new job and you're in the middle of a huge adjustment. We'll wind this down soon before it disrupts your life further."

The way she said "disrupts" like it was somehow an inconvenience, when it wasn't.

She was looking at him expectantly. "Does that work for you? All of it?"

Did it work? Was this all he would ever want from her?

"One request," Pascal said. "Sex in your shower."

She moaned right there in the kitchen. "I can't believe I forgot that. Absolutely yes."

16

He didn't *really* live in the Alban house, and Pascal was sure every single woman occupying it knew it too. No one thought for a second it was true but he still had to walk around pretending it was. Like he belonged there.

It didn't bother him because he actually did not feel unwelcome. After discreetly moving his clothes from the studio up into Rose's bedroom, he had a quick late dinner right there at the dining room with Rose, and then they moved to the living room. He sat on the edge of the sectional, watching a home improvement show that was casting on the TV. Rose was on the other end, using her phone that was hooked up to a charger. Carly showed up and hung out for a few minutes, talking to Rose.

"I've quit my job," Carly was saying.

Rose looked at him pointedly and gave a small shrug, but didn't explain. Back to Carly, she sighed. "So that's why you're here. You've never been able to get this many days off."

"You didn't let me finish! I'm moving to another job, and

I don't start for another month, but it's—" Carly looked behind her and dropped her voice. "*It's in Hawaii.*"

"You didn't tell Mom?"

Carly cleared her throat. "Only you and your fiancé who's listening knows."

"Carlotta." Rose was shaking her head. "Mom has been wasting her time plotting on the wrong daughter."

"I don't know, I like how *distracted* she is with you. She barely has time to worry about me. And it's time, Ate."

"You couldn't have at least stayed in the same state?"

Carly groaned, and Pascal had a flashback to the young version of Carly, not that he knew her at all. Whenever he showed up, she was upstairs or quickly out of sight, and that was probably by choice. He did remember the long ponytail, the bike helmet. She was always coming in or heading out. "Pascal," she said, catching him paying attention. "Do you still see your parents every week? It's perfectly acceptable for a thirty-ish young woman to skip *some* weekends right?"

Pascal's parents had a social life, actually. "I don't see them every weekend anymore," he said. "But that's because they want to see my niece a lot more. They don't care if I don't show up."

"See?" Carly pointed at him triumphantly. "There are other ways to live. They can find other ways to entertain themselves and not obsess over how many hours Ate Annika and I log at the house. They moved us for all these advantages, they shouldn't punish me for actually taking them."

"*I'm* not the one you should be explaining to," Rose said. "And Pascal's parents have a grandkid, which is a distraction we haven't given them."

"But you're getting married, right?" Carly winked

theatrically, at them. "Are you providing a baby distraction any time soon?"

"No," Rose said emphatically.

"I don't think so—" Pascal started to say, until he realized that he wasn't handed the script for this and should let her take the lead. And yet, they weren't exactly contradicting each other.

"No?" Carly was a little surprised.

"*No.*" Rose said. "No kids. Not from me."

"Huh." Carly turned to him. "I guess you're okay with that?"

"I am."

"*Huh.*" Carly said, shrugging. "Interesting. Maybe you're right for each other after all."

And that meant *what* exactly? Why wouldn't he be right for her sister? Pascal almost objected, almost asked what she'd heard, almost randomly started talking about the innovative education company he'd been *invited to lead* but then Rose's mom appeared at the bottom of the stairs and they all stopped talking.

For a second Tita Ramona was close enough to the living room that he could see her give them a little nod of acknowledgment. Then she turned and headed to the kitchen. She did that again on the way back to the bedroom she was staying in upstairs.

He didn't know any of them well enough to know what they were thinking but maybe in their own different ways they were waiting for him to slip, make a mistake that would open the door to the conversation Rose was trying not to have. Joke was on them though because this was a comfortable house, that he was sort of familiar with already, and Rose was indeed queen of this castle and she wanted him there. And he hadn't blown the cover just yet.

Still, hanging out with Carly too long might lead to a slip-up. Pascal made a vague gesture with his phone. "Heading up," he told Rose.

She smiled and pulled him in for a quick kiss like this was absolutely normal and they did it all the time. "Sure."

Then it was late on a Saturday night, and he was there in her room. Just him.

As mutually agreed, she'd locked her valuables, and gave him access to a drawer on her dresser for his own shit, and the key to its lock. She'd set up a new basket in the bathroom with fresh towels and toiletries, new toothbrush and everything. And when he was done with that, he saw that she'd re-folded and placed on one side of the bed the flannel blanket he made sure to bring up from the studio. Pascal guessed that was his side now.

Tita Ramona and Annika and Carly could be suspicious of him all they liked, but he was going to enjoy this entire experience.

He didn't mean to fall asleep before Rose even made it back up to the room on his first night ever on her bed but everything was so *comfortable.* Pascal had been scrolling through Netflix trying to choose a show to watch, then he was waking up when Rose slid onto her side of the bed.

"Hi." Rose whispered. The room lights were off now but he could still see her, still get all the sensory signals that she'd showered and dressed into sleepwear and he'd missed all of that. "Sorry—go back to sleep. Carly was talking forever."

"No no, I wanted to wait for you." If Pascal's brain would wake up fully and soon, he'd be able to explain why, but it was slow going. It was everything—the soft light from outside, the nice smell of shampoo but it was everywhere, the blanket now wrapped around him. "What time is it?"

"Past one."

He could tell that Rose was very carefully setting up her own blanket and he wanted to say she shouldn't have to worry about disturbing *him* on her own bed, but the words were not completely there and he also doubted if he was just reading it all wrong. And she was actually talking.

"...I mean how does she think that's going to end? She should just tell them right away that she's already made the choice. I would much prefer that my mother have some other life to fixate on if only for a few days. She can't even give me that? But Carly has always been that person. Gulatan forever. But oh my God you don't need to hear this now. Go back to sleep."

"It's okay, really." Pascal pushed a leg out from under the blanket in case that helped break the sleepy spell it was having on him. "I didn't want to spend the first night on your bed just—sleeping ahead of you. It's weird."

"Why, Pascal? Was there something you wanted to *do*?"

"I meant say good night. That's all." Pascal laughed. "We can share a bed and not do anything. Like on *Love Island*."

"*What?* What's *Love Island?*"

"It's this reality show—anyway these strangers are on an island and they choose who they want to couple up with and they usually start spending the night on the same bed but it's a room with many beds and everyone's there and—" Look if she didn't know it by now it wouldn't make any more sense if he explained it. "Anyway I only meant to say, yes, I don't take sleeping on your bed as an invitation to have sex every time. We can just sleep."

"Like on *Love Island*." It was a clear laugh at the end of that, and not just his sleepy brain imagining it.

"Yes. Good night, Rose."

"Good night, Pascal." Then, after the length of a long sigh, "Do they make out before going to sleep on *Love Island?*"

"Rose, how about let's forget I mentioned that as an example because it's not the best one anyway and I can't believe I even used it—do *you* want to make out before going to sleep?"

"Yes, yes I do," she said.

And then that beautiful, comfortable *everything* was closer to him, against him, wrapped around him. Her lips soft, teasing his mouth with light minty nips. They kissed like that only for a moment, too quickly it got deeper, heavier, his fingers on the back of her head and into her hair, her hands clutching his back then his hips.

They only did just kiss that night—but they kissed a lot. The kind of kissing that left Pascal's lips tingly and completely exhausted. The kind of making out that just ends with mutual surrender and whispered "good nights" and a surprisingly satisfying sleep.

17

Rose was very aware that not all families operated like this. She'd seen the ads with the tearful video calls at Christmas, had heard of overseas-family group chats active with photos of births, graduations, birthdays, all that. She was pretty sure those were sincere tears and happiness. She felt that too—of course—but when fundamentally disagreeing with a parent about her future, the best way to deal with it was avoidance. And she'd had over a decade of practice.

She was such an adult.

Annika: *Where are you? Mom wants to go to QC for lunch.*

Rose: *Errands! Out all day. Go do your thing, don't wait for me.*

Annika: *Ate. Come on. It's Sunday.*

Rose: *Enjoy yourselves!*

Annika: *You can't avoid her the entire time.*

Watch me. Rose thought that; did not text it.

Never mind that she ordered groceries via an app, or that there was a three-month-old washing machine in the renovated backyard, or that her subscription fresh produce was just delivered the other day. If she wanted to waste a lot of time, she was in the right city to do it. Rose left her own house early that morning and went to the grocery store, dropped off her laundry somewhere, went to the organic food market and looked at fruits. She spent all day spending way more time than necessary on every single errand she could think of. Pascal had been out all day but she didn't ask where he'd been. He got back in late that night, said something about getting something fixed at his place, but she couldn't remember all of it. She did remember the nice make-out session before she went to bed.

And then the next day, a Monday, she actually scheduled meetings. She chose a café at Six 32 Central for a morning catch-up with a friend, then the al fresco dining area of a salad-and-chicken restaurant for a lunch meeting with her accountant. She also bought a new journal, ink for a fountain pen she hadn't used in a year, considered buying a new coffee machine and let the sales clerk demo three different models to her before she ordered three packs of coffee beans instead. Anyway, she had a dozen or so more stores on this block to wander into before it got dark. This was a newer part of town and nothing her mother was nostalgic about. It was not likely that they would run into each other here.

However, it was more than likely that she would see her fiancé. And she did just that at four in the afternoon, in front of a café (not the one she had breakfast at or the seven others she had passed as she walked). "Rose?"

"Pascal."

So, she *knew* this, but Pascal was an attractive man. In a different setting and even among this well-dressed corporate Monday crowd, her eye landed on him even before he said her name, and she stopped walking. That blink of an eye might as well have slowed the universe. Rose felt her body warm up, again remembered what he smelled like when he got into bed. She knew that now. It didn't even take that long really, but her room was so completely hers that anything new was immediately catalogued by her senses. Senses that tingled as his face lit up with recognition. That smile, his mouth forming her name, the several steps in her direction. And then the kiss.

The kiss, right there in the middle of the business district. Honestly Rose didn't even think it was strange, she was probably half responsible for it, but as it happened, and was happening, and kept on happening, her brain reminded her that they were outside.

Rose started laughing. "Sorry. I didn't ask if we can make out on your coffee break."

He touched the side of her lips with his, before pulling away. "Unexpected but welcome."

"Why, is it a bad time?"

"Just Monday. The usual." Pascal shook his head and turned around, and Rose noticed the three other people waiting for him, likely his co-workers, audience to their very public display.

"Go back to work, boss. Are you their boss?"

"Not really, but they should act like it anyway. Are you on your way back home?"

"Oh, *no*. I need to stay out here until I know for sure my family made other dinner plans."

"But it's hot out here. You've been walking around all this time?"

"I had meetings. I bought coffee." Rose lifted the tote bag from her coffee source. "This is absolutely what a grown person does instead of tell their mother they don't want to have dinner together."

He flicked his head in the direction his co-workers were heading toward. "Want to hang out at the office?"

For all the ways that people scared her about turning forty, Rose was happy to report that a couple of years on the other side and things felt fine. She felt great, even. "Great" wasn't just about physical activity but she had friends who were way sportier and they seemed to be doing fine. Great was a state of being okay with herself and despite the physical changes, the weight of responsibility, and knowing her parents were getting older...she often forgot her age actually, and felt like she had always been this person. Felt like she finally was the person she had been trying to be.

What reminded her of time passing was seeing other people.

Already established: Pascal looked great. Looked hot. Was absolutely no longer the teenager who was noisily opening the gate at the house, or grabbing a sandwich from the kitchen on his way out.

In the office of Pisara EdTech he was the boss, even if he downplayed it. As soon as they all stepped into his workplace, occupying half the third floor of this new building indeed only a few blocks from home, Rose could sense how he both attracted attention and respect. The seas practically parted for him.

Then she watched him chair a meeting and there was all that grace, confidence, occasional smiles that kept him approachable but he was obviously still the most experienced and knowledgeable person in the room. Rose had intended to sit in the air-conditioned Instagram-cute office for a few minutes and then make her way out into the shopping center again, but ended up staying there, watching him, waiting through two quick meetings and a training session, parking herself on a stool and working through her inbox from there.

Before she knew it, the sun had gone down, and she let out a medium-volume squeal when she realized that she had distracted her way out of dinner with her family that night. Another day down.

One day at a time.

Pascal was the last to leave the office. That was what he did—closed up every night, at least while Pisara was starting up in the new location. It explained why he got home late. Rose had assumed he was having dinner with friends, or whatever else people who stayed out until late did.

"Is this going to be a school?" Rose was picking up bits and pieces from the office, the notes on the little blackboards and whiteboards, aesthetically pleasing Pinterest-but-real-life cork boards that had notes about students, and courses, and training, and goals for classes delivered. One entire wall was devoted to printouts of press and various other online coverage. Some of it was familiar, found when she was doing that quick background check on him. Pascal usually being interviewed, being head of operations and all. While the space was roomy and pretty, it didn't seem like it would function as an actual school.

"We'll offer training here, and studio services," Pascal explained. "But the idea is that they won't have to *be here*. We can package the classes as video, or stream them. They can touch base several times if they want to, and we can give them study space if they need it."

"So...like homeschool. Distance learning."

"It'll remind people of all of that, whatever they're familiar with. We've started the rollout with corporate training because that's the background of the founders, but then they brought me in to handle operations and also focus more on developing support for grad schools, then undergrad, then maybe if I'm not completely exhausted, K-12."

"That's a *lot*." Rose whistled. "I get why you wanted to move nearer. There's just way too much to do, right? You'll want more predictable, less stressful days. No commutes."

"Absolutely. Do you remember when you worked really long days and nights every single day? I don't."

"Oh, I remember, and opted out. I have a little notebook that has a list of my worst days at work." Other people had a gratitude journal, but not Rose. She compiled evidence of her career being unhealthy and looking at the list reminded her of the good decision it was to completely change paths. "I have not added a new entry to it in a long, long time."

"Becoming the boss might have helped."

"I *know* but that doesn't prevent us from meeting people we don't want to work with, right? Still, I haven't really hated anyone so much for them to make an appearance on a new entry. Thank goodness."

That was a privilege of being older though, and collecting good will and achievements all her life. A younger version of herself would never have been able to just cut people off.

"Then what?" Rose asked him when they were back on street level. It was after eight p.m., and the restaurants at the ground floor of this building and the two others beside it were all full. "Is it this crowded at dinner every night?"

"Every freaking night."

Rose was familiar with how crowded Six 32 Central could get on the weekends but this was an entire city block of full restaurants at dinner on a Monday night. From the looks of it, probably the same situation at the next block and the next. "How do you eat?"

"I buy a sandwich and take it home."

"There's a *lot* of food at home. Amendment to the conditions: You can eat or cook anything that's at home. This is ridiculous. A hundred restaurants and nowhere to eat when you're coming out of work."

"Imagine coming down to this and then taking two more hours to get home? No thanks. Your house saved my life." Pascal sighed and Rose could almost see the long day he had right there in his shoulders, his back. He'd been hiding it because he had to be *on,* and co-workers could see. She saw him deflate the tiniest bit, add some slack to his spine.

"There's still a lot of leftovers from the party with the titas," Rose said. "That's our dinner. Let's go home."

18

When they got back, the house was dark. Beside him, Rose gasped, squeezed his arm. "They're not home yet!"

"If they're anywhere outside of the village they'd be back late, because traffic."

"And if I head up to my room now, I won't see them today at all." Her pace quickened and when they got to the front steps she practically skipped. "Bring dinner up to the bedroom!"

"What?"

She had to yell back the instructions because she was already halfway through the living room. "Look around and heat our dinner and bring it up! With plates and everything!"

"Rose—"

He didn't even get to ask her what she wanted; she was already gone.

Which left him alone in the kitchen, where he apparently had all the power now.

This was a *nice* kitchen, okay. The Cortes family hadn't

been the big-kitchen type. The best food was restaurant food, and anything in the refrigerator or cupboards was meant to enhance it. Banana ketchup, for the takeout bucket of fried chicken. Spiced vinegar, for the grilled fish his dad would pick up on the way home. In college, he had learned to skip breakfast and have lunch and dinner at school. The exception was the occasional snack here, at the Alban house.

Pascal pulled the refrigerator door open and helped himself.

It took three trips to bring everything up to Rose's room but by the time he came up with the liter bottle of root beer that she'd asked for, she had set everything up on the balcony. She'd pulled out a table and some stools, arranged the rice and ulam he'd packed in those serving bowls with lids, set down the red plates and mismatched utensils in their respective positions.

'This what you wanted?" He showed her the bottle to check, with the flourish of a sommelier presenting tonight's red.

"*Yes.* Pop it open, let's eat, let's eat. You don't mind root beer, do you? It's your fault though because you got the crispy pata. I always have soda with crispy pata."

"I can get behind that," Pascal said. "This all right with you? Too much?"

She was giggling as she poured. "A little bit much, but you made good choices."

He'd chosen crispy pata, chicken afritada, broccoli with oyster sauce. Leftover garlic rice. A small plastic container of leche flan. It had been like Christmas in that refrigerator, all those choices, all the possibilities. His standards for a feast were not that high and he also mismatched this meal. But she liked it.

They'd just started eating when the gate made the sound. Pascal only needed to peek over the railing to see the van and the people coming into the property.

Rose did the opposite and dropped her head. "Is it them?"

The way they were sitting, she wasn't so visible anyway —and it was obvious they were home—but this was what the whole avoidance plan was about. "I see your mom and sisters."

"Anyone else coming in?"

"No."

"Ah, shoot." Rose seriously looked like crouching her head was making her invisible and it was not happening. "They might look for me. We're busy, okay?"

"We're having dinner."

"Yeah, but this looks like something they'll barge in on! They'll do that. Carly did that all the time. Someone's gonna knock any second—"

"We could just not answer the door—"

Knock knock. "Ate? You here?"

Pascal would laugh but if they happened to hear it, it would ruin Rose's cover, not that she'd decided on one yet. Rose bit her lip and suppressed a laugh of her own.

Knock knock.

"You really don't want to see them at all?"

Rose shook her head. "They just came home from seeing our relatives. Those are the titas *and* the titos. They would have been asking Annika and Carly why they aren't married. They would have grilled my mom about me and you. They're going to be transferring anything they absorbed tonight over to me, and you because you're here, and no one deserves that."

"We can't hide here forever."

"We just need to make it through the night. They'll get some sleep, vent their fumes to someone else!"

"Ate?"

Rose got up from her seat, moved closer to the door. Not that she actually did anything; she just stood there with her hand over her mouth, smooshing the laughter that was almost getting out.

Knock knock.

Rose moaned.

Pascal's breath caught in his throat. It was *that* kind of moan. Rose really did just walk up to the door and released a sound that was a *lot* like what she'd sounded like when having sex and he happened to know it for a fact.

The knocking stopped—because it was impossible to not have heard that from the other side of the door. Rose moaned again, punctuating it with a whimper this time, and even *that* Pascal recognized.

The next sound was footsteps walking away from the door, and heading down the stairs.

Rose pretty much skipped back to the balcony and took her seat again, a triumphant look on her face. "Well, that worked."

"Rose, that was impressive."

"Yes, very mature of me." Like she hadn't just made sex sounds, she dug back into her dinner. "I'm at that level of not wanting to talk to them right now."

"I could have helped you."

Rose's face lit up in a naughty smile. "You would have moaned at the door?"

"I can do that—or help any other way."

"I'm sure you've been in more, um, respectable relationships where they're not hiding with you in a room and scaring their family off with moaning. Sorry about this."

"Rose." She said those words and they absolutely did not apply to him. Pascal thought that this was absolutely fine. Kind of enjoyable. Why *hadn't* he ever been in relationships where he'd needed to hide and make sex sounds? He had been doing it wrong all this time. Or hadn't found the exact person who—"Please. This is fun. Everything about this is fun." *Don't fuck this up, Pascal.*

"Did you see that there's paella in the ref?"

"I saw it but I wouldn't have paella with this. Crispy pata and chicken afritada and the broccoli with oyster sauce, I mean."

"Yeah, good call. But you can have paella tomorrow if you want it, if no one else eats it tonight. Oh wait—take the paella to work as baon. I'll put it in a little lunchbox for you."

He started to say no, it wasn't necessary, but also remembered that it would save him a trip downstairs and a queue at some crowded restaurant. "That would be great," Pascal said. "Love being engaged to you."

"I'm a catch."

"Statement of fact."

She said it, and his response was quick because it was just *true*—and then they both winced as baggage wheeled itself in.

Pascal didn't believe he'd ever be one of those lucky lotto winners but this was a pretty good situation he found himself in. Not just the house or the food or the sex or the actually having someone to talk to on the walk home—whatever it was he could offer, she seemed to appreciate. It was—nice.

To show up not needing to be ready with an apology for something he hadn't realized he'd forgotten. But was his comfort happening at some cost to her?

"Rose," he said. He hated that his voice sounded concerned. Obviously she didn't need it. Obviously she knew how to protect herself. But if she wanted to talk about it, he was fine with it.

"Pascal."

"You're all right with this, aren't you?"

"Pascal, please. You mean the fiancé thing? It was my idea. And everything after."

"Have you ever been worried that someone will take advantage of you?"

"You mean are people hovering around because they want me as their sugar mommy? I'm not worried, but I'm very aware."

"Has anyone bothered you?"

Rose shook her head. "No."

"Okay then."

"No one has *bothered* me but they're very close to it. When I'm here in Manila, *I'm* the woman who's a certain age, who's got a house and a savings account and people think anyone dating me needs something from me. But when it's my family introducing me to some US citizen, it's the opposite. I'm the needy one who'll have to prove I love someone I just met because the marriage will get me a green card. None of the above. Kind of hate it."

"We've established that I can totally pay rent, right?"

"Yes, established." Rose shuddered. "I still remember when *I* was the young thing people were suspicious of. It never fucking ends."

"Everyone sucks." Pascal almost wished he'd quit and joined Pisara earlier. Spending most of his career as an academic and then starting a new career at thirty-nine was not that impressive when being introduced to many, many titas and titos. They had seen it all, judged it all. He didn't even own a house. "But you know you're great and they need to mind their own business, right?"

"Pascal." It was very mild but he could see it, that hint of delighted surprise. "It's nice to have someone on my side."

"I'm a catch."

"You *are.*"

19

"Oh come on, you do *not* fucking garden!"

Well, Annika was right. Rose had someone come over regularly to tend to the front lawn and didn't actually take care of the plants herself, but so what? Hanging out at the garden first thing this morning—where she could be alone—seemed like a good idea at the time. It reminded her to schedule the next appointment with Kuya Ed the gardener, and she was pleased with how the new vines on the concrete wall looked. They'd put that together as a project so they could have an interesting backdrop for future product shoots, and Kuya Ed had designed a detachable wooden arch and curved vines around it. It made the plain wall so interesting all of a sudden and it might be ready to be used by the time the next collection needed to be featured on the site.

But yeah, Rose didn't *really* garden. Still, she touched a leaf on a potted fern. "You're seeing me right here doing gardening with your own eyes!"

Rose's sister stepped out onto the porch, still in pajamas, mug in hand. "I have actual friends who are into gardening.

You know what they do all the time? Talk about their plants. Take photos of their plants. It's all over their social media. Their plants have names and I get photos sent to me even if I have no clue what they are. You don't do any of that and I talk to you every week!"

"Just because I don't talk about every single thing doesn't mean it's not being done. Some people don't broadcast their lives twenty-four-seven."

"Yeah, like how you're suddenly engaged?"

Annika Alban, middle child, had not always been like this. In fact, growing up it had been Rose who sounded like that, would have her hand on her hip demanding Annika tell the truth about something. Over their regular conversations, Rose knew Annika had needed to grow up quickly, and assume panganay functions as soon as they moved. That meant from age nineteen she'd had to help their parents figure out paperwork, banks and loans, healthcare, all the things that needed to be re-established in a new country...and then do it all over again for herself once she'd finished her college degree. At thirty-seven, she was doing well in her IT job, and was still unmarried, but their mother wasn't hassling her about it as much. Annika was already a US citizen, so.

"I do lots of things I never talk about," Rose said.

"Oh, it's obvious what it is you *do* with your fiancé, Ate." Even from a distance, Rose could see Annika's eyes rolling. "You're being really stubborn about this."

"About what?"

"You don't need to keep lying. Mom left early this morning with her friends, they're spending overnight at Tagaytay and will be back tomorrow."

Thank God. Thank God that Rose's mom had such loving and attentive friends who were always ready to take her on fun trips, was what she meant. "That's...good for her."

"Ate Rose."

"Annika. Did you eat the bibingka? I saw some on the kitchen table and someone needs to eat that today."

"We're here for just ten more days."

See, to Rose that sounded like way too many days, but on the balikbayan side of things that was going to go by in a blur. "Exactly. Those are precious days being wasted worrying about me. I'm obviously in no need of worrying over."

"You're not going to have a proper conversation with Mom?"

"About what?"

Annika gasped. "'About what' she asks!"

Rose had enough of fake gardening time. "What for?"

"All of this is so unnecessary and if you were both just honest with each other about what you really want—"

"Oh, no. Not the honesty. I've been honest about how I feel and what I want for a long time, Ans. She doesn't believe me, but I don't blame her for things she has nothing to do with. She can make a little hobby out of planning how I'll get my green card but I don't have to participate." Rose blinked. "Is that what you wanted me to do? Is that what I'm supposed to talk to her about?"

"I didn't say that."

"Then so what? She makes these plans and I keep doing what I want anyway. There's no need to have a conversation. Let her enjoy her trips and hanging out with her friends."

"Because I get to see her put herself through this and you don't. I don't know if she knows for real you're never going to take her up on it. *You* call it a hobby but she truly thinks she's working to save you from your situation."

"That's on her, not me."

"I'm the one who's expected to be emotional support over there if you don't settle things with her here and now. Come on, help me out."

"And that's why my engagement news works, okay? This is the closest she's come to accepting that it won't happen the way she wants it to. Even if I've said so for a very long time." And it had to be through a ruse, but go figure. "Enjoy your visit, Annika. We just need to distract and stall."

ROSE SPENT an entire day thinking about this and still came to the conclusion that her plan was the superior one. An "honest" and "open" conversation with her mother kicking up arguments Rose had been saying for years? Chaos, tears, and blame. A ruined vacation. Pretend engagement? Well wishes, entertainment, and family gatherings with a confidante and shield present. She knew what was the better choice.

Surprisingly, a lot more sex than she'd expected too.

"We have work tomorrow," she said, realizing at two a.m. that it wasn't the best decision maybe to have sex again if Pascal had to be at the office by seven. Where was the Rose from just days ago being all cool, he could sleep on the same bed as her and they didn't have to do it every night? Laughing at her now, she was sure. Still, Rose had control over her schedule and could push her day back an hour or two. Pascal couldn't possibly start a long day with a narrowing window of sleep but it was his cock, hard *again*, that she could feel on her back. "We should just spoon. Like on *Love Island*."

Pascal's laugh was a warm tickle when his chin moved

against the top of her head. "They don't just spoon on *Love Island*, please stop using that reference now."

"You started it."

"I regret it entirely. Don't worry about my work—it's just going to be there. I'm a boss by now, for God's sake. We decide if we want another round at two a.m. We deserve it."

Did she? The past few days felt so...decadent. Even the undercurrent of worry about where she stood with this man, something she was conditioned to worry about, wasn't there. It wasn't there because *she* set the terms and he had accepted. Was that all? Was it that easy? And then more than one orgasm a night was allowed? What was this life?

"I know we deserve it," Rose muttered, still honestly a bit buzzed from an earlier orgasm. "We work hard at it." She felt a lazy nibble at her earlobe and shivered. "But I also love sleep. I'm sure you like sleep too."

"I'll come back after the morning training and nap. Really nap. How about that?"

"I guess I could start work a couple of hours later."

"See, there are solutions for anything."

From behind her, his hand slid over her waist and touched her clit, softly parting her folds. Just one finger, teasing up and down, around her clit, and back again, until it was clear to them both how wet she had become. He knew by now how long it took. Not very long, really.

"Ready?"

It was obvious but he always asked. "Yes."

A moment of delay as he dealt with the condom, and then settled his hand on her thigh, opening her legs up slightly so he could enter from there, from behind. The stroke was long and slow, and took her breath away as he filled her. He pulled out, and pushed in again, hands finding her breasts, teasing her nipples. Rose's eyes were closed, but the sensations were everywhere. Hands, fingers, his tongue on her shoulder. This was a good angle, an almost dangerous feeling—each time he thrust she felt *that* kind of fire, a spot being stroked just *right.* If she had been on her knees or standing she would have gotten so weak and collapsed completely. Thank goodness for late night laziness and the safety of a strong bed. *Just right* became not enough, it had to escalate, and Rose pushed back against him to feel more, get it faster.

"You're rushing," he said. "We don't have to rush. You feel good all over. Everywhere I touch. I can keep this up all night if you ask me."

That was impossible. Rose wanted to argue with him about their age, their bodies, eventually they'd need more lubrication, eventually he'd need release, it was *impossible* to keep at this for hours. But more importantly, she didn't want a slow and steady thrust *all night.* Even if each time was perfect. Even if she was crying out every time he filled her. Something was missing, she couldn't even see him, couldn't hang on to him. She turned her head toward him and opened her mouth, and he swallowed her next cry into his kiss. And that was so much better, but not enough. She pushed back, into him. "Harder."

"Like that?"

"No, harder. Faster."

"You'll come."

"I want to. Give me what I want, Pascal."

"Always."

He increased pressure, thrust faster, and the orgasm that drew out was one of the best she'd ever had. She felt lit up from inside. Not at all drained, or tired, but awake, and when he said he was about to come she pulled away from him, moved, and told him to come in her mouth. They'd barely enough time to peel off the condom when his release began, hot liquid on her lips and in her throat as she sucked him.

Rose let go after one last lazy lick, rolled back to her place beside him as they caught their breaths.

20

"Huh."

"It really is mine." Not that Pascal really thought Rose didn't believe him, but it was funny seeing her wriggle into the passenger seat of his car, yes his actual car, the Civic he owned but hadn't used since he left full-time teaching at Anselmo Graduate School. Funny to see Rose as a passenger or a guest, really. He guessed that she was shaping the seat to her comfort, letting it familiarize itself with her.

"Oh, I can tell. Something about it smells like you."

"Literally the cologne I use. There's a little bottle in all my bags. There's probably one in the dash."

"You have a cologne? What is it?"

"You can snoop in the stuff I moved to your room later."

"It's nice that you have a cologne."

"I also have mouthwash. I used to teach four days a week."

"They probably liked you the most."

Pascal shrugged. "I did okay." Consistent positive evaluations from students—or minty fresh breath—did not necessarily guarantee a path to full professor, but he already bored her with that rant. And already told himself he was done talking about it. "Also handy for the good first impression when meeting all your relatives tonight."

"I hope you're not worried about that!"

"Should I be?" The obvious answer was he shouldn't. Not really engaged, not really about to marry into this family. Who cared what they thought of him? He knew all of this, and was sure to hear the same from Rose in a second, and he still asked it. Still selected his best pants. Still let her pick the color of the Zora/Maya shirt he would wear (brick red, and he really did like them, he should buy a bunch). And still left work early so he could swing by his place and get his car. The car he hadn't needed since he moved to Rose's because he could walk to work.

"It shouldn't matter, it's Teresa's night." Rose had stopped wriggling, possibly because she'd won, and the seat was now conforming to her perfectly. "So this is my cousin who's moving to Canada and what we do in my family is we have these really nice dinners as a send-off. We don't see each other for Christmas anymore, but we do for weddings, funerals, and despedidas."

"I'm glad this is a despedida."

"Yeah, good timing for us, huh? It's tough to bring a new boyfriend to the other times—weddings and funerals are way too intense. This is just a fancy sit-down dinner and maybe titas and titos asking you questions. Nothing you haven't done before."

"What do I tell them about your ring?"

"Oh." Rose flexed her fingers and looked at it, a lovely bright star on her finger. She'd worn it every day since they started this ruse, pointedly showing it off at the dining table or in casual conversations with her mom.

"You can just say you asked me what I wanted and bought it for me."

"That sounds legit."

"It is—I literally did see this and knew I wanted it." She stretched her hand, so Pascal could see the ring even as he drove. "Every now and then I buy jewelry for myself, but not a lot of rings. Then when I was having some earrings cleaned, I saw this, and asked to see it. The jeweler tried to sell it to me as an engagement ring, that I should 'tell my boyfriend' to buy it for me. They tell guys that an engagement ring should be equivalent to two months of his salary, do you know that?"

"Yes, I do," he said. "Popularly attributed to a DeBeers marketing campaign, but the multiplier changes every time I hear it."

"Does it sound like a two-month deposit on an apartment you're about to lease, or is it just me?"

"Well, when you put it that way, it doesn't sound all that romantic."

"To be honest, that really got me angry at first, and then I ended up thinking about it way too much. I mean, I was there and interested, why can't she just sell it to me? Why the performance of telling me to tell my man to buy it? I already liked it. I could have been asked to buy it. But also—why would she tell me to spend this much money on a rock? Suddenly it made sense to me, in a weird way. There's so much meaning attached to this, and it's not just that it's beautifully designed, and that I want it, but the cost of it also means something. That I'm *meant* to think about it long and hard, and not just purchase it on a whim. And then I thought of the last thing that I bought for myself that cost two full months of my salary and if I don't count international trips, then there's nothing. I have never decided to give myself something worth two months of my income.

"Until I bought this." Rose pulled her hand back, closer to her, and inspected the stone with a pleased look. "But I actually do buy jewelry, so it's not completely ridiculous a purchase for me."

"And you've never used it? It's like your mom hasn't seen it before."

"Oh yeah. I didn't tell anyone I had bought it. It *looks* like someone proposed to me, you know? And I had a feeling I'd get these weird questions, because some people think there are things you should wait to be given, and not get for yourself once you're able to. This is one of those things."

It had been a while since Pascal drove, but it came back to him pretty quickly. What also returned was the feeling of being in the driver's seat. Of controlling his mobility. Of owning the machine that took him places, and deciding his fate with each turn. Tonight, all of that was in her service, and every time it was clear that he was useful, and appreciated, but not really needed. Not absolutely necessary.

Once again, exactly what he asked for, right? He had too much on his mind to handle being needed by someone else. And he got to decide how much to be involved, and it looked like she truly didn't care either way; she'd survive with or without.

Pascal wondered if he'd found it, the perfect committed relationship for him. Ironically, unfortunately, one that required no commitment but the fake one.

Still, he could state the objective fact. "Rose, you deserve that and more."

"You're very kind. Love being fake-engaged to you."

Absolutely no argument there.

Pascal wasn't going to remember everybody but the point was to appear like he would, so he switched on his professor mode and said everyone's name after being introduced, and made sure to give good eye contact when shaking their hand. This "fancy dinner" was actually at a hotel function room expanded for fifty or so guests, many of them—Pascal was surprised to note—older than he was. Most of the people were in their fifties, sixties, seventies even.

"I kind of didn't expect to be among the younger people here," he whispered to Rose as they navigated the room to their table. "These are all your relatives?"

"Oh. Well, it's the titas and titos who love this thing, so they really won't skip a despedida if they can help it," Rose explained. "Of course *we're* tito and tita age now too so to a younger person, *everyone* here is old. But it's also, hmm, many of my cousins in my generation are living overseas, or don't have kids. We haven't contributed to adding young people to the reunions, so to speak. Do your parents expect you to have kids?"

"I'm someone's favorite tito and ninong, but that's about it."

Rose smiled. "Vivienne, right? How is she?"

"She's great, and surprisingly tall now."

"I have, like, ten inaanaks. Kids of my friends. I've sponsored diapers and formula and Kumon and ballet lessons, one time helped pay for a major medical procedure—my mom said I could have raised a kid myself with all of that energy but I know it's not the same." Rose paused and waved. "Teresa's coming over."

"Oh my god, *Professor Cortes*?"

A few surprises for Pascal: Teresa cousin of Rose was not

in their age group, which he had assumed for some reason. Instead Teresa was in her late twenties, *and* his former student at Anselmo. He didn't remember every student anymore especially when outside of the campus like this, but it had to have been within the past five years.

Teresa hugged her cousin and stood in front of Pascal with curious glee, holding her hand to him offering a professional handshake. "Ate Rose, you're marrying my MBA prof? Oh my God, let me just—I need to let this sink in. This is *so* unexpected!"

Her not-so-little outburst had gotten the attention of the titos and titas around them and he saw Rose's lips freeze in that composed smile for a second. Unexpected could be another way of saying impossible.

But Teresa seemed happy. And confused. They could work with that.

"He's like the hottest prof, Ate Rose. I mean, it's not like we had all these hot profs to choose from but Sir Cortes, you really were the hottest one there. People wondered if you were seeing anybody but we didn't know, no one ever saw you dating."

"Because it would have been inappropriate," Pascal was quick to say.

"Oh well, regardless—I did not expect this but it's *so* fascinating. Sir Cortes, Ate Rose is such a role model to all our cousins, especially to me. *She* paid for my MBA application, do you know that? This career path I'm on and the opportunity I've gotten is because of her."

"Tere." Rose was shaking her head. "It's not all *because* of me. You don't need to exaggerate."

"I'm saying true and nice things! Sir Cortes will want to hear them."

"I do," Pascal agreed genuinely.

Rose blinked at him. "No need to do that, Pascal and I are already engaged."

"But that's precisely it! I'm kilig that you're making her happy!" Teresa sighed. "I have never thought anyone deserved to be with Ate Rose *forever* but you could be a good contender. This information is so exciting. I'm going to tell my MBA batchmates all about this tonight. Enjoy the dinner! Excuse me I'm saying hi to Lola June."

Teresa skipped on over to another table quickly, and Rose was left to pick up where that left off.

"She really is overstating it. I don't have that much influence on their lives. I wouldn't want that responsibility." Rose laughed sheepishly. "And I'm pretty sure my mom's generation talk about me with pity, they always considered me someone 'left behind.'"

"She was a good student," Pascal said. "I'm going to believe her."

"You're supposed to be *my* fiancé, dude."

As soon as they took their seats, servers attended to their table napkins, served hot soup. "I'm guessing they were expected to follow the path our parents were on. Get married, have kids, send them to school, ask nosy questions at reunions for decades..." Pascal paused, satisfied when Rose snickered. "Seeing you around being yourself would have been such a refreshing and inspiring thing for them. Reminds them that there are other ways to live. I remember when my sister became that for me and others in my family."

"Because she had Vivienne and chose not to marry the dad?"

Tana went through a lot of firsts, at least as far as Pascal's relatives were concerned. First to study abroad, first to become a single mom, first to be in a long-term relationship but remain unmarried by choice. Based on how his own titas and titos treated his singlehood with concern and disdain, he was sure they speculated about Tana's situation more and with harsher judgment. Still, it didn't bother her, and she had all his support. "That, and everything related to it. She's always been following her own path."

Rose nodded. "Tana is like that, and she's very consistent about it. I don't even think of myself as being that brave but I guess it's all relative. Like, even being just a little different is brave to someone."

Based on what he'd been allowed to see, he would argue that she was braver than she was letting on. But Rose wasn't done talking.

"...It's not fun, being the one who gets to be the example, so others feel better about being brave too. We get tired." Her hand, the one with the engagement ring, reached for his. "We get tired and want the quiet too. And maybe we'll do things for the appearance of being on the same path as everyone else, just so the questions stop."

The gem blinked light into his eyes, a reminder of his place.

21

"Walk with me to the cake shop, Pascal."

"Yes, Tita Mona."

On the surface, the interaction looked warm and absolutely natural. Tita Mona was smiling, and the hand she placed on his wrist was gentle. Pascal looked around him and didn't see Rose; she hadn't gotten back yet from the bathroom. He fell into step behind Rose's mom, leaving the dining hall and making their way out to the hallway and toward the café and cake shop on the other side of the hotel.

He had been summoned.

They made it to the café and took a cursory look at the cake display for maybe a minute, before Tita Mona addressed him directly.

"Pascal," she started, "I realize that you're never going to answer me honestly about this, and also you and Rose are very loudly declaring to your entire household how involved you are. I can't seem to have a proper conversation with her about it, so I will have one with you. I don't actually care if you two are really engaged. As long as you're not married, her petition is not a lost cause. You can play house here all you want but immigration is still an option for her, as long as you're not married."

"Tita, I—" Again, Pascal wasn't sure what to say. "All of that is Rose's choice."

"Of course it is. Rose has every choice under the sun and how about you? What do you have?"

"Me?" Pascal wasn't supposed to want anything in this arrangement. Sure the terms were through a verbal agreement and subject to interpretation but he was very sure that what *he* wanted was the lowest on the priority list. "I'm fine."

"What happens to you when she changes her mind?" Cake display ignored, Tita Mona's eyes were on him now. "All it takes is for her new business to have a bad year, or she wakes up one day and wants to start a family. This 'relationship' works for you for now but what are you going to do when she wants other things?"

"You're assuming that I won't want those things. Or that we won't decide them together."

"Pascal. *Please*. Based on everything online about you, you're some sort of celebrated bachelor and now you're almost forty and I'm supposed to believe that if my daughter suddenly wants marriage and children *you* will be there for her?"

"Tita—you shouldn't just believe what you read online. You can ask me. I'm not some stranger."

"Right, and what kind of honesty am I getting from you and Rose right now? I'm talking to you about this *because* you're not some stranger. Obviously I care a bit more for your welfare than someone I don't know. And that's why I'm saying that you should talk to her about this. Imagine falling in love with her only to find out that she's leaving—and you know it's always a possibility." Tita Mona gently pointed in the direction of the dining hall with her chin, to Rose and Annika and Carly speaking to some guy. "That's Arnold Delgado."

Pascal shrugged. "Is he someone you'd prefer she be with instead?"

Tita Mona folded her arms. "Arnold's a dentist, the son of my dear friend from high school. He has a practice in San Diego. He just happened to be in town this month and I told his mother to tell him to stop by tonight, meet my daughters. Look, he's here."

"Very nice of him."

"He's here because he understands what we're all trying to give Rose. I don't know what she's been telling you about her plans but as a family we've been talking about her move for a long time. She knows this is going to happen. If not by my petition then another way. If she thinks she can bring you to a family gathering so she doesn't have to make the decision, it doesn't work that way. It's not fair to you either, if you don't know what it is that you're signing up for. Have you thought about this, Pascal? What happens to *you* when her papers come in?"

If only he could say that their arrangement wasn't even going to last beyond his lease. Rose definitely knew that Pascal was going to perform as fiancé for a limited time only, and made that very clear.

"We should get the cake you want and head back there, Tita," Pascal said, as a non-answer. "And if Rose prefers to be with him for that reason then—then it's her choice."

Tita Mona rolled her eyes. "How can I be happy that she's with you, when you talk like this? Like you're not invested at all. Or I just don't understand your generation anymore."

22

"Arnold! Oh my God. You were like, in diapers when we last saw you."

Rose said that and then Annika, Carly, and even Arnold laughed like she'd been joking. No, the diapers bit was a fact.

"Ate Rose, you can't help it, can you?" Carly said through laughing gasps. "Arnold is an actual man."

"A dentist," Annika added.

Oh, Rose knew exactly what he was meant to be, when out of nowhere Arnold Delgado, Tita Chloe's son, appeared near the end of dinner, seemingly just to say hi. The past decade or so had led to many people like Arnold dropping by to say hi, sometimes in her own home, often with some kind of food gift. Rose had taken maybe one or two of them seriously, in her twenties. These days she was seeing barely-thirty Arnold Delgado showing up to say hi and it was now customary to shut the whole thing down as soon as possible.

"Ate Rose, you look gorgeous, as always. I'm glad I got to see for myself, at least. Even if you will never marry me for a green card." The best part was when they were aware of this and didn't expect her to participate. "And they're saying you're engaged, so...congratulations?"

"Didn't you walk into this place five minutes ago? How do you know the chismis already?" Rose shook her head.

"That's enough time to get news. It's the first thing they told me."

"What does your mom want from us?"

"I think she'll be satisfied with a photo."

"We can do that." Rose hooked her arm around his, and leaned in for the selfie that he took with his phone. For a second, she checked if her sisters were around and would join the photo, but they were somewhere else now. So she smiled, and he snapped two cozy photos under the flattering hotel lights. And Rose saw him promptly send one of the shots to his mother.

"That's it," he said. "Family obligation performed."

"I'm so sorry for this, Arnold. Where were you supposed to be tonight? It's Friday and the traffic has to be terrible."

"I don't mind, I made plans to meet friends here at the bar." Their arms still linked, Arnold tapped her arm affectionately. "It's nice to see you, anyway. I have to admit that I was curious—the way my mom talked about you, it seemed like you're actually more open to this kind of thing now."

"Green card marriage arranged by the St. Mary Manila Rositas Forever batch? Still a no in the year 2019, to be honest."

"All right then. Walk me to the bar?"

"Sure. How's, um, dentistry?"

It was fine, and he was doing well, and sometimes when she had this conversation with someone her mother sent over, Rose would check if she was throwing away a good thing. Was she rejecting every single person because she didn't want marriage at all, or just didn't want it this way?

Because unlike no-divorce Philippines, there would be divorce in a US marriage.

She would think about it and then cycle back to no. It wasn't about the right or wrong thing. Many people had made a different choice many times, and they made those choices for their own happiness and freedom and whatever else they needed. Rose sensed her family wanting to peel away layers and see to the core of her choices, like they might be able to influence her if they knew what it was they needed to say or do.

The truth was, Rose evaluated these guys one at a time, in the moment, and then didn't think about them again. Arnold was just fine, and decent enough, and good-looking, and she knew his family, but she wasn't really in the mood to go through everything with him.

"What are you going to tell your mom?" Rose asked him. She didn't know Arnold as an adult, she realized. "I mean, don't tell her I rejected you. You're very eligible and you grew up to be guwapo. Tell her I said that."

"Thanks. I'll tell her you're engaged. That should give you a little break."

"Why did you agree to do this for her?"

They'd reached the hotel bar, one level down from the dining hall. They'd gone down the spiral staircase arm in arm to do that. "Rose, I'm single, and I was curious. I wouldn't have minded exploring if we had something."

"Arnold. You can't be serious."

"Why not? No one else they sent your way told you that?"

Maybe one or two of them would have, if Rose had given them a chance to go through the motions. "If you're looking for a relationship, you shouldn't waste your time on me."

"I would not have considered it a waste of anything. Even if you decided I'm not worth it."

Rose laughed. "You have a good attitude about this. Better than mine."

"But you've found someone, so everything works out." He pressed a quick kiss on her cheek before she waved him off. "They just want your happiness, I think. And now that you have it, then they can leave you alone now."

"Yay me. It was nice seeing you, Arnold."

They wanted her happiness, but it could only be the kind that they had.

Rose saw what she and Arnold looked like as they walked through the hotel, knew that even this idea was only a ploy. Arnold's mom was her mom's dear friend but she had a suspicion that the match was okay with them because divorce was a possibility. What if Arnold actually loved Rose? What if she loved him? Then the loyalties would shift, and she would be the "spinster" taking advantage of him.

None of the above.

PASCAL LOOKED DISTRACTED, on the drive back.

See, Rose noticed it, and as soon as she thought of it she told herself to calm down. Why did she even think that? And so what if he was? She really didn't know him that well. A week of him in her bedroom and two other weeks in the studio didn't mean she got to be an expert on his moods.

Still.

"Did my mom say something?" Rose said.

Pascal laughed. "Are you psychic?"

"No, just aware of repetitive patterns. I wondered if she talked to you privately while I was talking to other people."

"She told me..." Pascal's voice really trailed off there. "She told me it doesn't matter if you're engaged or not. If you're not married, then you could still be petitioned."

Of course Rose's mom would pull that card. "Well, yeah. And you know that even that isn't stopping her. Because I could marry a citizen, or get a job that comes with an employment visa, whatever that job may be. It's their generation's idea of helping." Rose sighed. "And I shouldn't be this ungrateful for the attention. For some people, it's all they ever hope for."

"But you've already said no thank you."

Maybe it was that, because she had always said it in versions of "no, thank you." It was hard to clearly and irrevocably say "no," when her own country was the way it was, and things could go sideways at any moment. It was easier to not say anything, or say thank you and ignore messages forever.

"Did she get to you?" Rose asked him. "Did she make you think that if you really cared about me, you'd let me go?"

Pascal shrugged. "But we're not really engaged. It doesn't matter what I said."

That landed heavy, like a stone. She replayed the words in her head and it was all true, but the way they sounded was not at all what she expected to hear. Or feel. "Well...if we had to keep up the appearance that you cared about me then it would matter what you said."

"Oh, I kept up appearances. Of course."

"What did you tell her?"

"That I support you, and staying here is your decision. Stuff like that. I stuck to the script."

"Then cool, because that's *all* you need to do." Rose was not a snappish person but that sounded almost sort of snappish. God, she hoped he didn't notice. She hoped she was just suddenly more sensitive and was misreading the tight tones and body language cues in this enclosed space. Because she wasn't psychic, and had never even been in a relationship that would come close to an engagement.

Maybe people had off days, and bad moods, and it had nothing to do with this current situation and what she was doing and saying.

Still, Rose was noticing things. It was hard not to, after their week-long insta-relationship performance. She'd agreed not to monitor his routine—and she didn't, she really didn't—but couldn't help but note how he stayed mostly out of her way when they got back to her house. She was tired, so she just took a shower and sat on her bed, and she only saw him again when he came back to the bedroom, and then sat at the desk to use his laptop. She did not get a bedtime snuggle. She did not get a good night.

Nothing wrong with that. There were going to be nights like this. There were going to be whole days like this, even during his time as her fake fiancé.

This is exactly what you wanted, she told herself, closing her eyes to sleep.

23

Pascal remembered why he hung out at Tana and David's. His sister and the senator had only started living together a little over a year ago, although they'd been seeing each other on and off for years. The visits to see his niece, coinciding with Pascal's frustrations with his career, relationships, everything—it led to his decision to Stop Fucking Around.

Because Senator David Alano's life and work was always more chaotic, on any given week. Any kind of problem Pascal had, David was likely going through worse, times ten. Yet the man had an air of calm that made it seem like he had it all under control. He'd already had to handle a number of emergencies and scandals in his term in office so far.

"You okay?" Tana asked, watching Pascal as he took a little too long to start eating. "Work doing well? The office will be opening as scheduled?"

"Yes," he said. "Work's great. How about you?"

Tana laughed. "You didn't watch the news?"

Pascal didn't have to watch to know that there would be something new and terrible, but Tana launched into a kid-friendly version of it anyway. Essentially, a word war with another senator's staff, lies somebody told the press, a corporation throwing its weight around to influence legislation. This had happened before but involved different people, and was a lot more stress than Pascal would ever invite into his life. But his sister and her significant other ate that up and still seemed to function somehow.

But they'd also known each other a long time, supported each other through so many life changes. Tana didn't want to ever get married—didn't even marry Viv's dad—and David was there for that choice even when it meant she didn't plan to marry *him*. They lived together, called what they had a relationship, and he apparently asked to legally adopt Vivienne. Their unconventional (for a Philippine senator) relationship was itself a source of scandal and rumor, but for better or worse they were sticking to their principles and not caving to external pressures. Good for them.

See, there were bigger problems in life than his own sudden, small crisis.

Yeah, was it small if he thought of it as a crisis?

He felt guilty, was what it was.

"Adult problems," Viv said to him.

"You don't have those problems, Viv?"

"Not like that."

"Thank *God,*" Tana said. "Her worst day was when the Wi-Fi was down for three hours."

"No," Viv said, matter-of-factly. "My worst day was when Reese and her mom got into that bus accident."

"Oh, you're right, darling," Tana's tone changed. "Of course."

Pascal did not expect his eleven-year-old niece to bring

that to the lunch table but she just did. "That's your best friend, right? They're okay?"

Viv nodded. "Yes, that was a long time ago, but I cried and everything. Anyway, the adult problems you talk about aren't like that. You're not really worried about people. You're not really hoping they'll be okay."

"We do work with some terrible people, Viv," Tana said. "We like to joke about it but a lot of this isn't funny."

"It's not funny, and it's difficult to make sense of what you're doing around them, if you're being honest with yourself," David added. Pascal didn't hear him talk about what he thought about his career really, but when he did he had this air of being close to done.

"You all tell me to be honest all the time," Viv said, her finger in the air, the arc she made covering every adult at the table. "But every adult problem you talk about has to do with someone lying. Why can't people just be honest about things and then everyone else just trust that they're telling the truth?"

If only. Pascal was spilling words before he could stop himself. "Because sometimes people can be honest and tell you what they want now, but it's likely they'll go through something and change their minds. And if that's very likely, you want to know as early as possible. So you can make better choices."

Viv blinked at him. "What?"

"You want me to repeat that?"

"I heard it, Tito Pascal, but I don't get it. You mean a person is honest with you *now.* Then you can already make a choice!"

"It's not that simple."

"How can they warn you that they're going to change their mind if they haven't done it yet?"

"Because adults are like that sometimes."

"Can't someone just change their mind and what they said before was honest and the new decision is also honest?"

"Yes, but—"

Viv was shaking her head. "Because you were saying I have to prepare you now for something that I might not do just because you're worried I might do it? But what if I don't? How would I know that now?"

"Good job, Viv," Tana said, eyeing her brother suspiciously now. "I think you're understanding the concept correctly but it's Tito Pascal who isn't being completely clear about what he's really talking about. Do you feel like sharing, Tito Pascal?"

To be quite honest? Pascal shook his head. "Not yet. I'm sorry. You're right, Viv. And Ate Tana."

"You were here last week and you didn't say anything about this. You sure? Do you need help?"

"I just need to think," Pascal said. "It's not—it's not like any of the problems you have. It's not evil staff and powerful corporations."

"Viv," Tana said pointedly, but gently, "We can accept that Tito Pascal is going through something but doesn't want to talk about it, and also that it might not be the same kind of problem as mine or David's work problems, but it's still important if it matters to him. Right?"

"Right. I hope you work it out, Tito," Viv said. "You know I just want you to feel okay."

~

"IS IT THE M WORD?" Tana had asked as he said goodbye, intending to drive back to Rose's place after visiting his sister.

Marriage? Did Rose talk to her about the—

"Mid-life crisis," Tana had added, before he spilled more beans. "I joke about it with David all the time but look, I know you made a pact with yourself to—what was it?"

"Stop Fucking Around."

"Yeah, I'm sure that resonates with you and if it motivates you then fine, but I always thought you were being too hard on yourself. You're quite the achiever. Your pace is a good pace. If they weren't recognizing your value where you were, it's good to go somewhere else."

"I'm not your kind of extreme achiever."

"My pace is my pace. And I don't think you want the problems I have. But hey—I mean it. We support you. We aren't keeping score and I never thought you were fucking around before. We don't have to talk about it now if you're not ready."

When did he suddenly acquire a problem? A year ago his biggest one had been what felt like double professional rejection, which capped off years of feeling stuck and unrecognized, and it was solved when he took on the job at Pisara. A few months ago, his source of stress was the daily travel from his place to the new office, solved when he started renting Rose's studio.

Suddenly that solution had opened up a new problem which was...

What was it, really?

It shouldn't be a problem.

It was nice of Tana to say that he hadn't been fucking around before, but Pascal often still found himself in this situation, his life revolving around a problem to solve. Or a problem to walk away from.

But she's not your fiancée. So it's not a problem.

Damn it.

It was late afternoon by the time he got back, and the house seemed quiet. He looked up at Rose's balcony and she was standing there, holding a drink in one hand and a book on the other. She raised the hand holding the glass and waved at him. He had parked at the curb and didn't honk the way others did, but the gate made a sound when he came in.

"How's Tana and everyone?" she said from up there.

"The usual. Evil staff and lying corporations."

"Isn't that everyone anyway?" She laughed. "I don't miss the work *at all*. Come up, I made drinks."

She was laughing and offering him drinks. Whatever this was, he liked that she was laughing and offering him drinks.

24

Before Rose's family moved, the balcony facing the driveway in the master bedroom had been barely used. Neither of Rose's parents liked hanging out there where it wasn't air-conditioned, so it had basic furniture that gathered dust, and was occasionally where they stored boxes and other junk. When Rose took over, that was what she had cleaned and redecorated first. It was an instant, easy way to claim a part of the house as completely hers. Currently, it was in its best state—the lounge chair, the pillows, a shawl for when it got cold, the small table, the attractive tower of plants, a small electric fan stored within reach, a plug-in lamp that zapped mosquitoes. The way the house was designed, the balcony never got direct sun, and when she was on the lounge chair she was low enough to not see anything but the tops of the nearby trees.

Eventually she would redecorate and repurpose every room in the house so it would feel hers, and not the rooms that formerly belonged to her family, but this balcony was the most comfortable and what she felt was truly hers.

And now, for the first time, she was going to have sex there.

Yeah, she really was out there on her comfy lounge chair, knees up and legs open, as Pascal pushed her skirt aside. She'd discarded her underwear right before this moment, possibly prompting him to proceed to this moment, and well, there was a first for everything. His head sort of settled against her thigh and he lazily ran a finger over her slit.

Rose *knew* no one would be able to see. Still, she might have looked up and around with a worried face for a second.

He still had most of her skirt bunched up in a way that she actually couldn't see his hand and what he was doing. She was only feeling the slightest of touches, a slow caress up, and down.

"You said no one's going to see us anyway," he reminded her. "You change your mind?"

"No, but—you know I was checking for drones. Flying by. Spying on us."

Pascal smiled. He was looking at her throughout this, his eyes on her face as his finger dipped into her, a little. "They'll need to zoom in and look under your skirt to see anything. But they'll know what we're doing."

His finger slid in deeper, stroked her inside.

"Rose. You know you're *very* wet right now?"

"I guess."

"Yeah?" Pascal slid his finger in the deepest it could go and Rose bit her lip to stifle half of her moan. He did that well, wonderfully. Smooth but also gentle. She felt like it really was for her. And then his head disappeared under the skirt and his tongue was on her clit.

Any spying drones would absolutely know what they were doing. Anyway they'd probably want to know how

Pascal was doing it, if they wanted instructions on how to do it well. Rose was melting into her favorite chair, again and again. He did not stop when she already came the first time; he just paused, let her resume proper breathing, continued to lean there in position idly stroking her thigh, her knee, her ankle. He asked her about the drink recipe, she might have answered by giving him a list of ingredients. Then he asked her if she wanted his touch again and she said yes, and he made her come *again.* And again.

THEN THE PLAN was to have sex in her other favorite place in the house, the bathroom. As discussed in their original terms. But when Pascal stepped under the rainfall shower and the hot water cascaded in what would have been heavenly pressure, he moaned like he was ready to come and she hadn't even joined him yet.

"I *know*, right?" Rose undressed slowly, letting him enjoy it. "You want me to leave you alone?"

"Don't. Just give me a second. *Oh my God.*" He bowed a little, let the water hit him lower in the back. "Oh my God, that feels so good. Oh, fuck."

Rose knew how good that shower felt, and also maybe why it was very specifically so very good. She slid into the spacious shower area behind him, touched the skin of his back, trailed her fingers down following his spine. "Is it muscle spasms? How long have you had them?"

"Forever, maybe. I mean I've had it treated occasionally but whenever I do anything now that gives relief it just feels so much better."

"If your work is a lot of standing up and talking, it takes

a toll." Her hand settled on the curve of his butt, and she nudged ever so slightly. "My turn."

Pascal stepped forward to let her take the spot under the rainfall but she didn't let go of him, instead wrapped her arms around him from behind and rested her cheek on his back. Held on to him as the water fell right where she needed it to. Stood there just like that, it seemed like for such a long time.

"Rose."

"Hmm?"

"Suggesting we defer shower sex to another time. I feel like I'm interrupting your intimate moment with it."

"Huh I was thinking the same about you. Okay, another time."

Or all the time.

A sudden thought. How strange.

They had sex on the bed instead, which was not a shabby plan B. It was great, even.

I like that. I would like that all the time.

As Rose was drifting off to sleep, she was thinking about being sexually satisfied on her own favorite balcony chair. And against the wall in the studio. That other time when he took her from behind. When she tasted him in her mouth. When he held her hand at dinner—all the times he held her hand at dinner. Driving her to the despedida. The straight-faced commitment to every conversation he had in her presence when he was being her fake fiancé. When he got plates of food from downstairs and heated it up for her. That first time he rolled up his luggage into the driveway. In the haze of happy hormones and sleep, Rose remembered a lot of things and liked a whole bunch of it.

I would like that all the time.

Even in her sleepy state she was aware she didn't usually

think like this. She remembered that she usually never said that—she had everything she ever wanted and needed. She had structured her life so she didn't need to be saved. Even if her family didn't believe her, she always knew. Every single thing on the list had been checked.

Maybe she was tired, or her brain was processing the day's overstimulation, but a little part of her let go. Told herself to be quiet. In the dark, she inched toward the warmth of his body, found space for her to slide into. Maybe he was awake, because his body moved to make room for her, looked for curves to hang on to. She didn't check. She didn't ask.

I would like this all the time—the thought formed, and then she slept.

25

"Pascal, that car outside is yours, right? I need to pick up a few things for"—Carly's voice dropped to a whisper—"the party tonight."

"The what?"

As far as Pascal could tell, it was only the two of them in the kitchen that Sunday morning. He was up before seven because his body clock did that to him, woke him up and made him hungry at that time even when he didn't have to go to work. He noticed the past week that the Alban family members weren't early risers, or that was just their jet lag and nights out taking their toll. He was usually able to have his coffee and quick breakfast by himself, then slip back up to the bedroom or out the door to work without bothering anyone.

This time, Carly wasn't just up but completely dressed and ready to go. "*The surprise party.* Mom's 65th. Remember?"

He only knew that he'd been invited but he didn't know when it would be. "I guess now I do. That's tonight?"

"Yes. I need to pick up the cakes and flowers and the

ulam trays. If that's your car parked outside, is that something I can borrow? That's okay, right? I mean as your future sis-in-law."

She was actually suggesting she would drive in Manila and he would just let her. "Have you even tried driving here?"

Carly giggled. "No but it can't be that different from driving in LA, can it?"

"Carly. You're joking, right? Do you want me to drive you? No, I'll just do it. Come on." Pascal's keys and wallet were already in his jeans pockets anyway. "You know where we're going?"

"We'll find it with Maps."

Pascal knew the area and wouldn't need precise directions until they got way closer so that was fine, but his mind raced as he tried to piece together why he didn't know that the party was happening that night. When was he supposed to find out? Rose hadn't mentioned it. Of course she didn't get to say anything last night—they were busy with other things and maybe the mood wasn't right to be discussing her mom's birthday. But then again it was Annika who even told him about it and that he was expected to be there.

"Does Rose know there's a party tonight?"

"She should." Carly was busy fiddling with the map app on her phone though. "I mean, she knows. We've talked about it. And it's her house. We've kept her out of the planning though, so she hasn't done anything for it. It's a bit much to expect her to throw Mom a party when we've already...caused all this drama."

"Well." Pascal shrugged. It sounded fair.

"You think we came here to mess up her life, don't you? Of course you do. You're always on her side."

He almost answered. It was odd that he actually had an

answer, and he might have really believed it. Whatever the cover story was, he didn't have the right to make any proclamations. "Do you remember Manila, Carly?"

She made a face. "Of course I do. I wasn't *really* a fetus when we moved. I've stayed in touch with some of my friends. And I've visited a few times! I'm not completely disconnected."

"Yeah, but you offered to drive. No one wants to do that."

"*Or* I suggested the more preposterous option so a good person would offer to drive me, and look at us now. I could be a genius." Carly was smug for a second and then dropped that for a somewhat serious peek at him. "Or you really are a good guy and you happen to love my sister and would do anything for her family, even drive her sister on a sudden errand. That's nice. I wasn't sure people like you existed."

"Carly." Pascal knew that the simplest way to keep up the ruse was to take the moments like this one, when actual family truly believed they were engaged, and just *not think about it.* They'd fallen for it! The only thing to do was not screw up. Really. *Keep it simple, Cortes.* "Your sister is—is very capable, even without me."

"I know that. Ate Annika and I, we know that Ate Rose will do whatever she wants. *You* are like a completely unexpected situation here, but I don't hate the idea. I have a good feeling about you."

Keep it simple, Cortes. "You barely know who I am, Carly. And Rose didn't mention me."

"Oh I don't *completely* trust you, it's not that at all. But if Ate Rose says she's happy then I see it, I see why. My mom and her friends have been a bit too invested in this green card marriage job plan for her for so long."

"No one asked them to stop?"

"Let me guess—your entire nuclear family is still here."

True, though. “Yes.”

“How does Ate Rose talk about it?”

“She said it’s harmless ultimately, like a hobby for bored people.”

Carly shrugged. “Well because they can’t *force* her to do anything, really. She still has to sign papers and do the interviews herself. She has to want to do it, and that’s their problem. Mom and her friends and everyone else—they can’t understand why Ate Rose doesn’t want their help. So they act as if she’ll eventually change her mind, because of course.”

“It’s been over a decade.”

“I know! But if you know people with aged-out siblings, you know they wait that long. All the time. This is common.”

“It’s 2019,” Pascal said. “Our options are different now.”

“Aw, Professor Pascal! Love your idealism. Ate Rose went through a phase of trying to educate my parents on immigration and border policy and I’m pretty sure her silence on that lately is because she is now extremely tired of talking to people who won’t ever really get it. If you *really* wanted to help her get them off her back there’s one thing you should be doing right now and you aren’t.”

Huh? What had they not yet done? He’d moved in and everything.

“Actually get *married*,” Carly answered. “Make it legal. *That’s* what will stop this ride, and you know it. Getting married in the land of expensive annulment and no legal divorce? That’s the abyss. You do that and they won’t bother her with their matchmaking ideas anymore. If you really want to help her then do *that*. Why are you waiting?”

26

"I thought you sent your laundry out?"

"Mom, oh my God." Rose did not expect the exact person she was hiding from to show up in the backyard laundry area. And she *did* send her laundry out last week because that was the excuse of the moment. On this day she had slept in and woke up to an empty house, and thought the laundry errand would keep her in the backyard and out of sight even if they had started to return. "Happy birthday."

She set the laundry basket she'd been holding aside and moved closer to her mother, and gave her a hug.

"Thank you," Ramona Alban said, equal parts surprised and entitled. "We missed you at lunch."

"Mom, they're your friends. And if they miss me they can drop by here and see me."

"When you aren't doing laundry, I guess."

For the heck of it, Rose did a large load of pillow cases and flat sheets just then. They had just come out of the dryer. With the right mood this was a chore she didn't mind doing; folding was relaxing in its own way. "They can come over and watch me fold, if they want to hang out. But this isn't what you want to talk about, Mom. How was lunch? Good restaurant?"

Conversations with her mother that weren't about visas and green cards happened before, did they? What were they about again? Surely they'd been able to talk about other things. It just seemed like that was so long ago and Rose couldn't remember them. The family had moved as messaging and audio/video call technology developed, and they used all of it. Rose also used to send lengthy emails about her work complaints and thoughts about her career.

They gossiped, that was it. Rose and her mom gossiped about celebrities and politics and people they knew. Once Rose left political comms and stopped following it, she had less to share. Her mom's own friendships changed and Rose became less familiar with the characters and maybe also lost interest in the drama when it was about someone's kids and nephews and grandkids. There was just a *lot* of names.

"Yes, it was a good restaurant." Ramona exhaled way more dramatically than that sentence needed though, and Rose knew that the conversation would shift back yet again. "Rose."

Rose busied herself fluffing a pillow case up in the air and then laying it flat on the surface where she did her folding. "Mom."

"I get it. I really do."

"Get what?"

"You don't want to live with us."

"That's not *it*, Mom. Paperwork decided this a long time ago, and I just...chose not to wait."

"But you've remained unmarried all this time," her mom said. "Even now, this engagement? It's not marriage. Technically you can still do this."

"Do what? Marry one of your friends' sons? Start a new career in another country in my forties?"

"That's what we did. Sometimes that's what you have to do."

Wait a second. Rose did quick math, and there it was. Her mom had been forty-seven when they moved. When they got the papers, and left the house of their dreams to Rose. Late forties, when she established her family in a totally new country, and navigated her way through jobs, and healthcare, and loans, and keeping a roof over their heads, making sure Annika and Carly were getting an education. Maintaining long-distance relationships with her dearest friends. And all the highs and lows that came with being Filipino in another place.

Rose's mom did all that. For herself and other people.

"Mom," Rose said. "I've said this before and I really hope you're able to just...hear it right now. It's your birthday. I really do mean it. You didn't fail me. You didn't abandon me, or leave me behind. I *knew* I wouldn't be able to go with you, and I honestly did not feel like my life was a waste. I've been happy, and I haven't been *angry* about your green-card matchmaking hobby because I've never felt that anyone was forced on me."

"Arnold *actually* likes you," her mom piped in. "His mom said. He really would date you if you were open to it."

"*Mom* no. I was saying—now if *you* feel that you failed me, I hope you realize that I don't blame you for how our lives turned out. At all. You've made choices that you felt were right for you and dad and Annika and Carly. And when it came to the help I needed here, you showed up for me too. You're here now for a few weeks and every day you have people wanting to see you—you can put your energy toward all of those people instead and I promise you, there's no need to find closure in somehow moving me to the US no matter what."

"But the door isn't closed, that's why I'm always reminding you of your options," she said. "Just so you know, it's not—it's not sayang."

There was a breakthrough happening here but Rose also couldn't help but flash back to the year they moved, what they both looked like then. A twenty-three year old and a forty-seven year old...Rose was closer now to forty-seven, but *felt* like the Rose she always was. How strange.

But also, how familiar.

Back then, she was bracing for independence because she knew it was coming. So many times she acted like a grownup because it was expected, and honestly? She was also just winging it. Making the best decisions she could, hoping for the best, learning from mistakes. Which led to wiser decisions, sure, but Rose couldn't argue that at forty-one she would never make a mistake. That she would never change her mind, even about this. Even if she'd spent almost two decades thinking it through.

It was all still possible because Rose wasn't *old*. At forty-one she could still feel young and uncertain.

Could still make mistakes associated with the uncertain.

Could still make brave choices associated with the young.

Ramona made a different, but also brave, choice at forty-seven.

And through it all, her mother didn't deserve to feel like she had accomplished all things but one. The guilt was so unnecessary.

Time to let it go. "I think what you'll need to do today, on your sixty-fifth birthday, is let it sink in that a marriage scheme is not what will make me happy. Can we agree on that? Walang sayang. My happiness is my own business. If anything happens to me because I've kept refusing your help, then it's my fault."

"It doesn't work that way. Of course I'll help if I can."

"Then help but in the way I ask you to. Find a new hobby for the rest of your retirement years. The plan to marry me off ends here."

"But what if—"

"Mom. I just said. Let me handle this part of my life, from now on."

Pretense of folding laundry forgotten, Rose felt her mom looking at her, and she returned the stare. Except it wasn't confrontational staring, not this time. It was...recognition. Rose observed her mother's face and took note of all the little changes in another person that somehow weren't transmitted on photos and video. She was sure her mom was doing the same.

"Fine," Ramona said. "And I do have hobbies. I did think this was something we had, just the two of us. Something we could plan together."

"We can just group-watch a reality show next time. Or I can finally learn to play mahjong."

"I'm fine, I have mahjong friends." Ramona waved dismissively, and Rose was relieved that she wouldn't have to play mahjong with her titas. Dodged one there. "So how do you explain Pascal then?"

"Oh. He's...we're involved, I guess."

"Not engaged? Tell me the truth."

Rose bit her lip. "Yeah, we're not really engaged. But we *are* involved."

"He really seems to be enamored, Rose. I've talked to him."

"He was pretending to be my fiancé. Maybe he's just a really good actor."

Ramona grinned slyly. Conspiratorially. "I don't know, hija. You know I've talked to him a few times, just the two of us. I don't think he's pretending about how much he cares for you."

"*Mom.*" They just agreed—! And now it was like she was starting a new scheme...? How did she do it? How did it happen? Before Rose could launch into a jumbled speech about leaving well enough alone, they both heard noisy happy activity in the house.

"Who's here?" Ramona had to know it was somehow for her. It *was* her birthday. She quickly kissed Rose's cheek and went back into the house.

Good talk, Rose thought, a conclusion left for her alone to process. But it really was a good talk. Maybe this talking—and listening—openly had something to it. Who would have thought.

It was near the end of this sudden balikbayan trip, but Ramona Alban's surprise party was as good a time as any for Rose to release that breath and just...relax. Finally just enjoy seeing her mother and sisters be in the house they used to live in, among friends and family who missed them. In the past few weeks, the house regained a feeling that it used to have, that energy of laughter and conversation and people. Rose did not love all of that enough to organize house parties herself, but she could participate and enjoy letting it happen in front of her, once in a while.

There were *three* cakes. One was "for the photos," a ten-inch round and hefty sponge cake, with macarons piled on top of ube buttercream frosting. Another was a rectangular vanilla birthday cake like what Pinoys had at parties when they were kids, but topped with a delightful cartoon version of Ramona. The third was a simple dark chocolate cake, still deserving its place at the table because it was a family favorite. There were festive flowers, trays of Filipino food, and Rose's sisters and cousins who'd amazingly defaulted to roles of arranging food, making sure everyone had a plate, taking away empty trays and replenishing dishes and drinks. Someone's playlist of '80s songs—heard on the street in the Philippines to this day—was casting on the living room flatscreen. People were finding their groups and mingling.

Rose was a little late for the festivities. When people started arriving, she had only just left the laundry area and needed time to get ready. When she made it back downstairs, early dinner had started, and over twenty people were already somehow there.

Pascal, too. *He* seemed aware of the surprise party and was dressed appropriately, and wow he looked *good* in a mandarin collar and what was the size of that shirt, because the way it hugged his chest—

Then she noticed that Pascal was with her mother. And she was showing him her phone? Rose did not pass go, went straight for them.

"...and he's head of operations at a—what is it again? A school?"

"Yes, in a way. Training and support for schools and other educational institutions."

"*And* he has an MBA and teaches at Anselmo. I'm sure his parents are very proud. He did well for himself, hon."

"Are you in a call with *Dad?*" Rose was horrified.

Mrs. Alban's grin was beauty-queen calculated surprise, and she turned the phone around so Rose could see her dad on the screen. "Of course I had to tell him about Pascal, your fiancé. So much chismis going around the world about you already and he's missing it!"

"Hi, Rose," Rose's dad said, three-fourths of his face occupying the main video screen. "You didn't tell me you're getting married!"

"Talk to your dad," Ramona said. "My friends want to meet Pascal."

See, Rose had enjoyed her peace of mind after their talk at the laundry area a little too much, and failed to close this loop. Also she wasn't yet in the habit of texting Pascal "where are you" the way couples did sometimes, so she didn't realize her mom would get to him first. Anyway, now the phone was in her hand, and her mom and "fiancé" were with a different group of guests.

"Dad," Rose said, slipping out through the front door to take the call on the porch. "How are you? How's Tito Ricky?"

"Everything's the same. You're getting married?"

"I'll call you later." Rose said, waving at him. "The signal's really bad out here."

27

Pascal helped Carly pick up the cakes, the flowers, and some of the party food. It was several hours worth of driving, and Carly was in calls with different friends for a whole chunk of that time. That meant his conversation wasn't required, and when he wasn't talking, he was thinking.

One of his thoughts was, how opposed was he to marriage again? When did that start? His parents had a great marriage, all in all. He just assumed they were lucky.

He also assumed he wouldn't be as lucky. That long-term love wasn't a dream, or something he needed. Even if his relatives had things to say, his parents didn't insist. *Why aren't you married yet* came up a lot when he dated, and he was always able to say with conviction that he didn't plan to, at all. He couldn't even imagine it. Every time he came close to a relationship, it seemed entirely disruptive to a very organized schedule. In fact, overloading the schedule to accommodate another person's time, needs, and goals. He'd only needed to check with himself annually if he was on track, but with another person? Daily calibrations. The inevitable "this isn't working out, we don't want the same things" arrived, and Pascal knew it was him.

He didn't do relationships. This was his life choice, many times.

He'd even told Rose all of this when he'd moved in—a recent witness to his state of mind just weeks ago.

Because why wasn't this terrible?

A week or so of playing house, sharing a room, meeting practically all her family, running errands with her sister, dodging the scrutiny of her mother—all while focusing on his new job and being able to still do that. Sure this was more of a simulation, but he navigated through most of it for real. He really did stay in her house, really did interact with her family, really did enjoy her company, really did look forward to giving her pleasure and receiving it too.

Maybe it's not terrible yet.

Maybe pretending makes it easier.

Maybe the pre-determined end keeps it from devolving into—

Into what? Into the thing that he and Rose said they didn't want?

If they could keep this going for X amount of time with some success, couldn't they learn how to extend that time, and in fact learn more with more time, and also find more factors that would keep this not terrible?

He was thinking about this for hours. He was thinking about it while he drove Carly, while he lifted boxes of cakes delicately into the car. While he got ready for this surprise party. And when he arrived, Tita Ramona wasn't just happy to see him but actively parading him around to all guests as her future son-in-law.

"When's the wedding?" someone asked. Tita Ramona shrugged and tossed the question to him.

"Rose decides that," he said, easily.

The guy who asked, apparently Rose's mom's cousin, laughed in response. "What do you get to decide then?"

This could have been a nightmare. Pascal was sure this was the very situation he was avoiding ever being in, hence the resolution and the rules. But he felt fine—this was a simulation, and it made him feel safe. Even when so much of it wasn't fake.

In the past, any relationship declaration felt like a promise. No, a trap. *He* didn't believe he'd ever follow through, so it was stressful to even try. But this situation right now? He was allowed to make declarations he might never keep. He was allowed to promise things. Whatever made the act more believable, sure. It wasn't a betrayal to say something and then take it back later. When Rose called this all off, it would be taken back anyway.

"The honeymoon," Pascal said.

The unexpected reply delighted his small audience. They immediately asked where the honeymoon would be.

Pascal began to remember really old conversations, snippets of the things Rose used to talk about, when they first met. When he was nineteen, and she was twenty-one and would never be interested in him.

"My friends own this nice place in La Union," Pascal said. "They receive long-term guests all the time. People who really stay there for weeks to surf, and eat, and sometimes even work from there. We'll stay for a bit, try all the restaurants. There's a great food scene there, and it can still be pretty quiet."

"Rose doesn't surf," someone said. "She's not the sporty type."

Was that an error? He didn't run this by her. But Pascal wasn't worried about being unmasked as a fake fiancé, not right then. "She doesn't have to surf. She can watch me do it.

Or do whatever she wants. I think she'll enjoy the community, and be inspired by all the artists and entrepreneurs there. I'll introduce her to my friends, because they have so much in common—you know, following their passions and being mindful of the good they need to do. A lot braver than I've been. They'll love her."

They were standing in a circle on one side of the living room, and Tita Ramona was still beside him, all the better to take him to the next group of friends. Tonight, she was different toward him. First of all, she was acting as if she actually liked him, which was nice. She was also "on," as both event host and center of attention at this party, and Pascal realized that she'd been performing all night. But right now, as she listened to him, she was thoughtful, and "off." Just listening.

"Oh my God," someone said. "I hate sand and the beach and I wouldn't want that kind of honeymoon at all but it sounds like something Rose would love."

Would it? He felt a slight regret because he probably wouldn't find out.

Only because it sounded like a great idea and he liked executing great ideas.

Surely he wasn't out here wishing a honeymoon plan he'd spontaneously made up from nothing was real.

"It's so perfect for Rose. You two are so lucky to have found each other," someone else said.

"Are you all done?" Rose appeared beside him, slicing through the little circle of people. "Can I borrow Pascal now?"

And that was it, the exit. Pascal smiled and excused himself, and then let Rose lead him away from his audience.

28

Rose didn't own a videoke machine; she wouldn't do that to her neighbors. Still, someone managed to figure out how to switch from a Spotify playlist to a YouTube playlist of '80s music lyric videos, and party singing prevailed. She'd give them an hour before shutting it down. Impromptu videoke time would be a good time to update Pascal without anyone hearing.

He hadn't left her side since she rescued him from her mom's turn around the room, showing him off. She would have mentioned something as soon as she took him aside, or while they were having dinner on paper plates at the kitchen island, but people were hovering around them the whole time. For the titas who were at that first dinner with Pascal, or the second one at Teresa's despedida, they were fascinated to see him again. A third appearance? Probably even the most skeptical of titas would concede.

They wouldn't have reason to suspect that this wasn't a serious and totally real relationship. Everyone saw Pascal holding both their plates, one in each hand, as they went through the buffet table that had been set up against the wall of the dining room. Rose was picking dishes for them both, and she seemed to know what he liked. They shared a stick of pork barbecue at some point. Of course they were a couple.

"Mom knows we're not really engaged."

"*What.*"

The front porch was empty—literally everyone else was singing inside—so it was their first private moment in hours. Even though people could see the outside through the large windows, and see them out there if they wanted to, they didn't need to play up the PDA. The way Pascal's arms immediately went around her waist, cradling her as he backed her into the nearest column and kissed her, *really* kissed her, for the first time that night. Not necessary, but they did that.

They were having this conversation with arms still around each other, her back still against one of the wood columns of her front porch.

"When did she find out? How?" Pascal asked.

"This afternoon. Right before the party. We had a nice talk, finally. Like mature adults."

"You mean right before she paraded me around all her friends and relatives as her future son-in-law."

"Yeah, I guess she wanted to do that. Consider it your birthday gift to her?"

The arms around her tightened ever so slightly. The next kiss she received was deep, and went on for an impressive amount of time. It was truly a moment. Rose had, frankly, never been kissed as the theme from the 1987 movie *Mannequin* played in the background, sung with gusto by a dozen or so voices. Maybe those who've had the experience could tell her if it was responsible for the extra *something* she was feeling.

And then the kiss was over, and Pascal stepped back, away from her. "So that's it, then?"

"That's...what?"

"Our 'engagement.' You don't need this anymore."

Define "this" because—"Well yes. The engagement. But it's not *over*, not *all* of it..."

"Right." He was shaking his head, as if shaking off a thought. She was not in the circle of his arms anymore but he hadn't let go yet, was gently clinging to the tips of her fingers. "An ex fake-fiancé still gets to see you, right?"

She nodded. "I'm right here."

"An ex fake-fiancé still gets to kiss you?"

She waited if this was a performance, and then he would kiss her, to prove that he could. But maybe he wasn't performing. Rose felt it again, how something was off with him but she wasn't sure what.

"An ex fake-fiancé still gets to stay the night?"

"*You* get to stay the night, Pascal. *You* get to...do whatever we want to do. Even if the act is over."

"Because it's true what they all say. You don't need any of this. Or me. I was just—checking. You might want to pack this up now that you really don't need it."

"I really don't think things have to change all that much...I don't understand..." *Wait a sec.* "Pascal. Do you *want* to remain engaged?"

Talk about things she never thought she'd have to say. But maybe it made sense, because asking him to be her fiancé wasn't on her bingo card for the year either. Once the door was opened to strange, it would follow its own course.

"I didn't say that."

"And you wouldn't, Pascal, because you don't even *want* a relationship. How did you describe it to me? You want to be responsible, so you won't even start one because you don't want it."

"I remember." He squeezed her fingers. "You don't have to remind me. Those are my words."

"What are you worried about?"

"Nothing."

That was absolute bullshit. But this wasn't the place or time to call him out on it. Did she even have the right to? What was she, really? Rose had only ever been taking care of herself, and rather than push, she released.

"I'm getting dessert," Pascal said, or something like it, going back into the house.

ROSE WAS outside on the porch by herself throughout "Make It Real" by The Jets, "These Dreams" by Heart, and "Can't Fight This Feeling" by REO Speedwagon. She checked the time, and figured she'd give the party singers one more song before she asked them to stop, on behalf of the neighborhood. Then "Total Eclipse of the Heart" started, and yeah that was a good song to end with. She'd let them have that.

"Ate, you're out here." Annika had come out of the front door and joined her. "I was wondering when they were going to be asked to stop."

"I'll go back in after this one and shut it down."

"Where's Pascal?"

Rose shrugged. "Inside, I guess."

Annika joined her where she stood, parking herself against the handrail. "Mom told me that you talked."

"And?"

"That you aren't really engaged, but she's not going to force the green card issue on you anymore."

"An actual mature and reasonable conversation. Are you surprised?"

Annika smirked. "I never believed you were engaged to him. Carly too, but she was going to get benefits out of it anyway. She made him drive her all over the metro to pick up food this morning, did you know that?"

"No." Rose laughed. "I don't think Mom ever believed it either."

"I mean, it was an interesting idea. But it wasn't necessary."

"Of course it wasn't."

"I'm not going to make excuses for how Mom has acted but I've always known you'll make the right decisions for yourself. I look up to you. Carly does. Our cousins do. What happened to you was random and unfair but you did everything you wanted to do anyway, and I've always considered that such an inspiration. Who cares what the titas think? If you want to remain single and here, then that's your choice."

"Hang on there one second," Rose said, as the party singers in the house wailed on. "I appreciate the compliment but don't make me out to be a hero. We know there are worse things in the world to randomly happen to someone, and that I have the house, and that you're all doing well, and Mom and Dad are okay—that's not something I consider a personal achievement. That's luck, and privilege, and I know life can easily go so very wrong."

"Yeah, but give yourself some credit, Ate. You've overcome major things too. And seeing how you're doing is an example, whether you feel it's lucky or not. Especially the staying-single-despite-all-the-family-pressure, that's been so good to see."

"Dear God my dating life is *my business*. I'm not your

single-life 'role model' to make you feel better about your own choices."

"You're telling me that's not your intention? The way you push back against all the titas looking to set you up? The way you've insisted to our own mother that you don't *need* anyone, all the time?"

"It didn't *look* like there would be anyone worth having all of that with. So there wasn't. It's that simple."

Annika batted her eyelashes. "I've always admired you *not because you're single* duh, but because life does throw you all the challenges but you always make it work for you. That's something we all need. That's all it is, Ate. It might seem small when compared to the world on fire but knowing that you will always do that helps get someone through a tough time. That someone is me, and maybe a few other people. I thought you should know that."

But she knew this, didn't she? Rose didn't need anyone to tell her that her decisions, though seen as different and difficult, were always valuable *for her*. Some people never got to do that for themselves, because something or someone would always demand to come first. Then it would become the way of things, to go through the next stages of life as dictated by someone else.

For some that would be easier or even comforting. For Rose, not at all.

If someone else being spectator to her life found inspiration in it, then...she couldn't tell them to throw that away. She'd be a jerk if she did that.

"Fine," Rose said. "I accept your compliment."

"Wow. Maturity! I love it."

"Well, something had to change after all this time."

Annika grinned. "You're right about that. I mean, this new challenge is interesting, can't wait for an update."

"What challenge?"

"You know, the one where you insisted you don't need to be with anyone, and now you suddenly have someone you like, someone you can be with, someone who took everything you threw at him and wants more? *How ever* will you deal with it? I can't wait for you to figure out how to make this work."

SINCE ROSE SEEMED to be on a streak of open and honest conversations, she figured she should do a few more that night before whatever it was wore off.

First, she told the singers that videoke time was over, and the birthday party festivities for Ramona mellowed somewhat into conversations where people made and served coffee, and they dug into all the cakes. Rose cleaned up a bit, but this event was by no means over. Like that dinner when her mom and sisters first arrived, she expected the guests to stay until dawn.

Pascal was not downstairs, though.

But she didn't need to talk to him right away. She stepped back outside and made the call in the relative privacy of the front yard.

"Tana," she said, when her friend picked up. "Did you want to set me up with your brother? Is that why you sent him to live here?"

"Good evening and *excuse me*, he was looking for a place to rent in the area and you have a place in the area. You also accepted a rate that was way below what you would have charged anyone else."

"Because you're my friend!"

"What exactly are you accusing me of?"

Causing a disruption. The words were caught in Rose's throat.

"Is everything okay, Rose?"

"Yes. I'm not mad or anything. I just—I need to process. I need information, maybe."

"What do you need to know?"

What *did* she want to know? What could Tana even tell her? Rose might have called expecting to hear confirmation that it was a setup, that Tana planned this, that she wanted her friend and her brother to date but didn't just say so. But that didn't make a lot of sense, and yes it was her brain looking for a place to shove the accountability for this. If only a matchmaking sister would take credit. But it wasn't happening.

Rose sighed. "Is he a good guy?"

"Did he do anything?"

"A lot of good things. Makes one think he might be a good guy. I need...confirmation, that's all. A character reference maybe."

"He's my brother, so I know him but I don't know *everything* about him. But what I know is he's been actively trying to be a good person."

"He told you about his resolution to stop fucking around...?"

"Oh that. You probably understand by now that in context, his version of fucking around is a lot different from someone else's. He's been evaluating his life on the basis of degrees he got and titles he was—or wasn't—given. On how he failed to be emotionally available for people he was supposed to be in a relationship with. He's not a *failure* failure. You know what I mean, right? We've encountered living breathing scum of the earth at work. I mean, I was just on the phone with one earlier today and it's Sunday."

Rose briefly flashed back to her work in political comms and shuddered. "Okay, I get it."

"That's what I mean. He thinks he's not good enough because he has standards. But really, he's a good guy. If I understand what you're asking."

"So you're not warning me to stay away from him?"

"No, because I see no reason to, but also, you're going to make your own decision on this anyway. I'm just trying to not make it awkward."

"Thanks, Tana."

"Anytime, Rose."

29

Should he pack up? Pascal stared at the drawer that contained his clothes. He'd pulled that open intending to put the contents into his luggage, but ended up just looking at it for a while. And then wondering if he was overreacting.

Tita Ramona never believed it anyway. Sure he did his best to not break character, but she had her eye on him and if she suspected shenanigans, then she was spot on the whole time, congrats. Annika as well. Maybe Carly was the only one who kind of bought it. The point was, he didn't have to keep staying in her bedroom. He could go back to the studio, back to his place, and...

And what? So what?

Did he want to move in? Like, *permanently?* He would be telling someone else in this situation that this was going too fast. It started as an act, for fuck's sake. Calm down, and figure out what being together looked like when pretending wasn't part of it.

But that was the point—

"Pascal."

Moments ago, Rose had come into the room, and he'd been too engrossed in the drawer dilemma to notice. "Hey. Everyone still partying?"

"Yes, they will be." She looked past him. "Don't leave."

Did she say—

"The conversation earlier got weird, but I want to be clear about it anyway. Stay here tonight. Stay here every night until my mom and sisters fly out, and then let's talk about what happens after. That is, if you want to. If you don't, I mean...can I call you? Ask you out?"

"Rose." What was this feeling? Relieved and joyful at the same time. Glad that he didn't have to make the tough call to offer to leave. At the same time, not afraid of the decision that had just been put off for a little longer. "Rose, I don't know about staying engaged. When you asked bluntly, my mind kind of blanked. I'm still not sure about marriage at all —but I didn't want to say the wrong thing."

"There's no *wrong thing*," she said. "I hate to say it, but we're old enough. We can say what we mean if we actually know what it is. I haven't changed my mind about ever getting married. We're not engaged anymore, and that's it."

"Okay." His release of breath was definitely a relieved sound. "Yeah, same page there."

"But you liked this? So far. Living here, with me. Doing all of it."

"All of it," Pascal said. "Dinner with your family. Breakfast that I have to serve myself. Talking to you about my day. Running into you at the coffee shop on my break. Walking back home together. I want all of it."

"Sex on the balcony?"

"In every room. Rose, what I just realized as you came in —we spent most of our time on this without an audience. Just you and me, here and anywhere else. I wasn't pretending as much as I thought I was." Every conversation with her mother and sisters and everyone else came up and he knew he had to correct himself. "I wasn't pretending *at all*. I do care about you. If you wanted to get that green card anyway, I just might ask Tita Ramona what my options are."

"Well don't open that door just yet. You might not know what you're inviting inside. And you just might be feeling...like your options are few now and you're rushing through the steps."

"No."

"No?"

"No. Did you just hear yourself?" Pascal gave himself a moment to look at Rose, and never felt more confident in contradicting her. "You and I don't have fewer options. Not because of our age. Not because of where we are. We've done just fine, haven't we? And we decide what the steps are, and how many, and we've done enough."

"You *are* a catch."

"You are too." It was the mildest way to say it. Perhaps he could do better. "But you don't have to take that—you can let me tell you and show you all the ways. I'm capable of more than what we've done so far."

"Pascal," she breathed, her hand on her chest. "Careful. That sounds a lot like a vow."

"Will you allow me to do this all, for you, for us?"

"Pascal."

"Will you let me prove to you every day how grateful I am that you're in my life?"

"Pascal."

"Will you let me explore with you every single way you experience pleasure? Because I'm ready. I'm willing."

"*Pascal.*" Rose's lips formed into the most beautiful smile. And then she said yes. "Yes, I will."

EPILOGUE

The next photo shoot for the Zora/Maya corporate separates collection only actually happened two months later, because of gloomy, unpredictable weather on the few days that Pascal had an entire day free. Good thing it was easy to keep rescheduling, because he was still living with Rose.

It was amusing to think of it that way—like he showed up for a five-week lease and still hadn't left yet, haha—but surprise surprise, Rose didn't feel like her world had completely changed. It didn't feel like her space had been reduced to fifty percent of whatever.

"This fine?" Pascal asked.

"Something's not right," Rose said. "Undo your top button."

"Again?" He was teasing but he did it anyway, undoing the top button of the shirt he'd been asked to wear. "Why do you even sew this on if you prefer I not use it?"

"For *options*. And different purposes. See? For this purpose, this is just better."

Pascal pulled at the collar to reveal just enough neck, a

peek at just enough chest. They had him on the porch, inexplicably reading a prop sheet of A4 paper, the least convincing memo ever. He braced a hand against a column and leaned his weight against it, forearms working.

And Rose's breath was stolen from her. Just like that. Still.

"Lord. Every single time. He looked perfect five adjustments ago." Bels—holding the camera—interrupted with exasperation that was only half kidding. Right, Bels was there. "But let's really do this without the eyeglasses from now on."

"Why?" Rose whined.

"Because there's glare from every possible angle and what matters is we photograph the *shirt,* Rose, not your hot professor fantasy."

"Why do we have to *choose*?"

Pascal laughed. Bels rolled her eyes.

"I'm happy for you two, I truly am," Bels said, "but it's Saturday and I would like to be done soon. And if we're done soon and I get out of here, you can be alone."

"Fine," Rose said. "No glasses. And I'll go back inside and start cleaning up. Just let me know when you're done."

"Best idea you've had all day, partner."

The dining table looked like a work table again. Months after the visit from her family and the parties, the house shifted back to being hers. Fabric on the tables. Pouches, tops, pants, samples and sizes. Her calendar was busy, and some days were tiring and rough. Like usual.

In no time at all, Bels was saying goodbye. Her friend picked up her bag, left the camera on the table, and said something about a date. Like usual.

"Honey, I'm home."

It was a joke. Pascal didn't do that often, but when he

did, Rose's heart leaped. She had a feeling one day it would sound regular, a statement of fact. Maybe one day it wouldn't sound like the sexiest thing at the end of a long work day, or the funniest reference to a time when they were faking.

Every time they talked about "them," Rose and Pascal agreed to take it a day at a time, and as days turned into weeks, and weeks turned into the past two months...

"Finally," Rose teased, turning around to find him right at the door, wearing his reading glasses again, full hot professor mode back on. "Long day at work, honey?"

"Yes, but I'm not too tired for you."

He was playing it up, but she believed it to be true. Their days could be long. They were learning together when each other's presence was restful, and when it was the opposite.

"If you're very tired," Rose said, "I'll help you with the rest of those buttons."

"That's nice of you. You might want help with *your* buttons."

"Oh, great idea. Why don't you start on that right now."

One time she asked him what was different now, why was he so good at this when he had been so hesitant to start.

Maybe I'm good at learning, he'd said. *And this is something I'm determined to learn to do right.*

That wasn't a full enough explanation. *But why us? Why now?*

That's the mystery, isn't it. I just want to. Do you want it too?

A mystery. *Yes, I do.*

The End

AUTHOR'S NOTE

In case you were wondering: the "aging out" that happened to Rose is a real thing. It's what happened to me, when a family petition filed when I was an infant was approved finally when I was 23 years old, and my status was determined based on the processing time that I had no control over.

My family went on to make a new life for themselves in Texas; I was in my early 20s and suddenly in charge of everything they left behind in Manila. But the similarities mostly end there. Without giving away too many personal details, I will say that I made different choices from Rose.

When you're "aged out" though, that becomes a thing that connects you to fellow "aged out" friends, and by staying in touch with them you get to see possible versions of your life. What happens next for someone in our situation has a lot to do with what they need, and what they have access to. I chose differently, Rose chose differently, other people can and will do their own thing. But I hope I was able to add a new perspective to a very specific situation that's used to pressure people into arrangements they might not want for themselves.

In 2002, the USCIS Child Status Protection Act went into effect, and that changed the way they calculated the age of a child whose family petition was being processed. That means "aging out" as I described in the story no longer happens as often. My "batch mates" and I are probably some of the last to have gone through it, in this way. This situation had very real "romance implications" for those going through it, because some petitions required people to remain unmarried. There are many stories of people who found love and lost love because of this.

Writing and producing a book in 2020 and 2021 is a different level of relying on people and for that I'm thankful for the help of Layla, Veronica, Tania, and Chi (core team for my books). Thank you, Kirsten and Dre for being our cover models, and thank you, Jo, for finding them.

Mina

ABOUT SIX 32 CENTRAL

Six 32 Central is named after "63" (country code for the Philippines) and "2" (area code for Metro Manila). The district as I've described it is mostly fictional, but based on real neighborhoods in Metro Manila. My plan was to write about characters who had chosen to live in "632" and how they were making the place better for themselves and other people.

Apart from the four main novellas in the series, I've written a short story called "Saved By Hope," serialized in the Philippine Daily Inquirer's premium digital edition in 2021. I may write a few more short stories, but *Totally Engaged* is the last novella-length book for this series. Ready to explore other "area codes."

Thank you for supporting the series!

ABOUT THE AUTHOR

Mina V. Esguerra writes and publishes romance novels. Her young adult/fantasy trilogy Interim Goddess of Love is a college love story featuring gods from Philippine mythology. Her contemporary romance novellas won the Filipino Readers' Choice awards for Chick Lit in 2012 (Fairy Tale Fail) and 2013 (That Kind of Guy).

In 2013, she founded #RomanceClass, a community of Filipino authors of romance in English, and it has since helped over 80 authors write and publish over 100 books. She is also a media adaptation agent, working with LA-based Bold MP to develop romance media by Filipino creatives for an international audience.

Visit minavesguerra.com for more information about her books and projects.

Six 32 Central series: What Kind of Day | Kiss and Cry | So Forward | Saved By Hope (short story) | Totally Engaged

Chic Manila series: My Imaginary Ex | Fairy Tale Fail | No Strings Attached | Love Your Frenemies | That Kind of Guy | Welcome to Envy Park | Wedding Night Stand (short story) | What You Wanted | Iris After the Incident | Better At Weddings Than You

Addison Hill series: Falling Hard | Fallen Again | Learning to Fall

Breathe Rockstar Romance series: Playing Autumn | Tempting Victoria | Kissing Day (short story)

Scambitious series: Young and Scambitious | Properly Scandalous | Shiny and Shameless | Greedy and Gullible

Interim Goddess of Love series: Interim Goddess of Love | Queen of the Clueless | Icon of the Indecisive | Gifted Little Creatures (short story) | Freshman Girl and Junior Guy (short story)

The Future Chosen

Anthology contributions: Say That Things Change (New Adult Quick Reads 1) | Kids These Days: Stories from Luna East Arts Academy Volume 1 | Sola Musica: Love Notes from a Festival | Make My Wish Come True | Summer Feels | Tropetastic Kindness Bundle 2021

BOOKS BY FILIPINO AUTHORS
#ROMANCECLASS

Visit romanceclassbooks.com to read more romance/contemporary/YA by Filipino authors.

Made in the USA
Middletown, DE
25 January 2022